M

The Story of a ~~Fisherman~~ ...t

Roger Penney

CRF PUBLISHERS

GOSPORT, Hampshire, ENGLAND

MOW

The Story of a Piratical Tom Cat

Roger Penney

First Published 2010

CRFPUBLISHERS
30 Leesland Road, GOSPORT,
Hampshire PO12 3NF.
ENGLAND

CONTENTS

Best Wishes

Roger Penney

ACKNOWLEDGEMENTS

Several of my longsuffering friends have read these stories. Then I chose those people who like animals and so, had they met the model for the hero of the tales they would have found him a place immediately deep in their admiration and their affections. I am grateful to them for having read and having enjoyed and approved. They also noted a few typographical errors which I have put right.

Writing about Mow the years have rolled back to my early youth and the strange something, a wonderful charisma and endearment which the large tom cat with piratical instincts brought to our small family.

So thank you to the following. Firstly to Mot, the archetype of Mow, who brought mystery and magic into our lives. Sadly it is more than fifty years since he fought his last fight and died shortly afterwards. Birmingham Parks Department may not be aware of it but he is buried at the edge of some of their land. I will not tell them where in case they want to dig him up. I will not allow him to be disturbed. The place was originally the back garden of our 'prefab' but has reverted to open land. If you are wondering why the venue for these stories, with wild ground and a little river running into the sea, has changed from the Industrial Midlands to somewhere near the ocean it is because I am an expat Brummy, who now lives on the South Coast, near Portsmouth. You might guess that I had the wanderlust and joined the Navy at a very young age, then settled down in what was once a maritime town.

Secondly, thanks to those long suffering family and friends who took the trouble to read the stories and who approved of them. Thank you Fraser, Phil and Graham; you have all been a big encouragement to me.

In particular I should thank my granddaughter Charlotte Penney but she is in a different category as she is a partner in this business and I look forward to publishing, with her, some of her writing, in the near future. Fraser is in the same category and both their criticisms have been invaluable. Theirs is the task of putting all this in order and then getting it ready for the printers, or to go 'on line'.
Roger P. July 2010.

FOREWORD

This is a small collection of stories about a cat. He was a real cat that really existed and though he did not do all the things in the stories he was just the sort of cat who might have done given the right circumstances.

He had white socks, a white bib and a white spot on his nose. He was very handsome and very intelligent and quite the charmer with the ladies. Human ladies fussed over him which he considered only his due. Too much fussing, unless it was by my mother, tended to bore him unless the fussing was accompanied by food. Most lady cats adored him.

There were people who did not like cats or were afraid of them. These he delighted to tease by making himself comfortable on their laps. And turning his rear too close to their faces for their comfort. He displayed real affection for my mother, who fed him, and for my father and I, who sometimes fed him.

As a feral male cat he had a large territory to patrol and we often met him when he was off exploring on his own. On these occasions he refused to acknowledge us, giving us a look which said, "I am very busy on important business and cannot be bothered with humans at the present. Please go away and come back when I am hungry, when I might deign to recognise your presence."

In the world of cats he was, for many years, the top alpha male of alpha males.

He died after his last fight to defend his title. We think this was the way he wanted to go, not with a bang, not with a whimper but with a howl of rage and a lot of feline bad language.

His favourite foods were fish heads, any other parts of the fish, bacon rinds cheese rind and assorted meat scraps. He also lapped up gravy, that is real gravy made from the meat juices of the Sunday joint, and liked a few small pieces of bread soaked in it. He always insisted that he should have a drink of milk from time to time.

After sleeping, his favourite activities were hiding under the rhubarb leaves to catch unsuspecting birds, surveying his empire from his special tree and fighting other males, notably a large male called 'Panda' who lived four doors along the street.

Dogs were very wary of him. The Spaniel next door always beat a hasty retreat when it saw him. On their first encounter Mot had scratched the spaniel's face severely. Ever after he was terrified of Mot. The incident of the Labrador really did happen but it was not a union official who brought him but one of my friends. Stephanie the Bull Terrier is fiction; I invented her as a foil to show Mow's own special intelligence and peculiarities which usually bewildered Stephanie. Dogs are not always the natural enemies of cats since if introduced when a kitten or even half grown as Mow was, they can become quite friendly. Staffordshire bull terriers in particular have strong maternal instincts. They are also good and very protective with the children of their family, being called 'nanny' dogs in earlier times.

One of my friends, who lives opposite me, has a German Shepherd dog. As a guard dog she is quite fierce but she plays happily with the two cats from next door and allows them the run of 'her' house. They may even be found all curled up together on the bed, the dog and the two cats.

The original Mow did invade the house next door and spent a night there exploring. He also marked his territory by spraying our neighbour's new trousers with his own specially pungent tom cat scent. How he managed to get into the airing cupboard we shall never know but he was adept at opening most doors. He did also find another neighbour's Sunday joint unattended in their kitchen and commenced eating it. The neighbour found him and chased him off before he had made serious inroads into their special meal of the week. They never allowed us to forget this incident. I think they believed we had trained him with his piratical instincts. We did not, he was a predator and all food was fair game for him. It was what came naturally.

Cats really are special. They can be wonderfully affectionate, especially to people who feed them and allow them special places to sleep. We ought not to be too cynical about this. Though my mother argued that our cat's brand of love was 'cupboard love' and so designed to open food cupboards, he did show pleasure (or greed) and, if food was in the offing, would run to us with a special cry of pleasure which my mother called a chirrup. It may be the practice of having cats neutered which reduces their capacity for affection. I know it saves a population explosion of kittens but modern (or post modern) politically correct cats are not the same as they used to be and few have the hunting skills and the fierce independence of the tom cat that our hero is modelled on. Perhaps it is something they put in the synthetic cat food that comes out of tins. The original would have looked with haughty disdain at what we feed our cats on today and would have stalked off to rummage in someone's dustbin, or to demand cream in a very compelling voice. Today's cats are very lacklustre compared with what they used to be; compared with Mow or with Mot his alter ego.

I want you to enjoy these stories. They might be fiction but they are about incidents which could have happened, or might have happened, or actually did happen. They are also an attempt at a preliminary study into cat psychology. Alas that particular subject is far too deep for a mere human like myself. It would require a cat of Mow's intellectual powers to do the real Ph.D. thesis. He, of course, would see it as a waste of time when there were much more exciting things to do like sleeping, fighting, hunting and eating while conning humans in between these essential feline activities.

Beware of the Cat

MOW VICTORIOUS

Mow yawned and blinked his eyes. He appeared still sleepy but he was a cat and they can come awake instantly. He looked about him and decided nothing had changed and maybe it was too early to wake up. He was about to go to sleep again when Stephanie the Staffordshire bull terrier spoke to him. "So you are awake at last," she said sarcastically. She could not understand that cats were animals of the night and liked to sleep during the day. Mow could not understand why Stephanie liked to be up and about during the day. Neither animal understood the other but they were quite happy sharing the same house and the same humans.

Mow yawned again and gave Stephanie the sort of look you give to your average mentally challenged garden gnome. "Dunno!" he answered in a bored voice. "Nothin' much goin' on, may as well have another snooze." He started to settle again, wrapping his tail round himself so the end covered his nose. It was not so much to keep his nose warm but that it was comfortable that way. Mow was a cat and did not see why he had to give a reason for everything.

Stephanie was not impressed. Having started something she usually saw it through to the end. Bull terriers are made that way, they hang on. "I really cannot understand you," she said. "Do all cats sleep all day? Mow stirred and thought for a bit. He was not really tired but sleeping is something cats are good at. On the other hand he knew Stephanie would keep on and on until her questions were answered so he decided to answer her. Being a cat he usually was able to turn most things to his own ends and conversations with Stephanie often gave him useful bits of information.

Not a week earlier she had told him about the new tom cat over the road. This gave him the chance to go to meet the new cat and to put him in his place. That is to make sure that he understood who was top cat, and who wasn't. The new cat soon learned his lesson.

Then there was the case of the ornamental pond in the policeman's garden a few doors down the road. Mow would have found out anyway because he kept a close eye on everything but it was nice that Stephanie had mentioned that there were fish there, obviously the policeman had bought them and thought them a good idea. Mow thought them a good idea too. If the policeman had been a detective he might have worked out that disappearing fish might be linked to the presence of a tom cat living nearby. Sadly for the fish population the policeman thought that all cats were well fed by their owners and blamed the herons who came from the Wild Grounds near the little river that ran into the sea a mile or so further on. No one ever saw Mow in the policeman's back garden but Mow had that contented look on his face every morning when he came to be let in. "Like the cat who got the cream," said the male human. The female human shook her head, she suspected it was fish.

There was no point in having a cat flap, Mow was too big. He was a giant of a cat. They, the humans that is, put out a box for him with a plastic sheet over the top to keep out the wet and some old blankets to make it comfortable for him inside. After his night's prowling and hunting for mice, or fish, as the case may be, he would curl up inside his box outside the back door and wait for the humans to stir and let him in. They always gave him a saucer of milk in the morning.

The idea of the box and the rain proof cover had been the male human's because if Mow did not have somewhere comfortable he would demand to be let in and that would mean waking the whole neighbourhood at five in the morning. Mow could be very demanding when he tried.

Mow thought for a bit and decided to answer the dog's question. Being something of a philosophical cat he hedged his bets and defined his terms. "It depends what you mean by cats," he said thoughtfully. "Then, of course, I have not experienced all cats. On the other hand most of the cats round here do sleep in the day and go out at night. Some stay in at night and never go out at all. I guess they are what you would call 'fat cats' but I don't count themas cats."

He paused for breath but Stephanie looked puzzled. Bull terriers are not the most quick on the uptake of dogs and, of course, dogs are not as quick on the uptake as cats. At least that is what cats think. For the most part dogs do not think very much; they much prefer their pack leader to do the thinking. In her case, Stephanie saw the humans as her pack leaders and she was content. As always when Mow explained something Stephanie was more confused than she had had been at the beginning when she had first asked. She sat and scratched herself as dogs do when they are confused. That is the problem with philosophy, as well as with cats, who are mostly philosophers of the Post Modernist kind. If you try to argue with a cat your words will develop legs and start running off in all sorts of directions you had not thought of and had certainly not intended.

While Stephanie enjoyed her humans and looked up to them, Mow thought of them, as he thought of everything else, as existing entirely for his own benefit. Some people are like that though I should not expect you are because those sort of people do not enjoy reading stories. They most certainly do not enjoy reading stories about cats. Whereas Stephanie belonged to the humans, in Mow's view of the world the humans were just there and, as good humans should, they provided Mow with the good things of life, like milk, chicken and, 'oh bliss,' fish and even cream.

Of course there are some cruel and unkind humans. There was the young man down the road the other way, not far from the post office. He was the sort of human who took pleasure in hurting small animals. Mow might have been small-ish. He was smaller than many dogs. However as cats go he was a giant. All cats are agile and strong for their size. Mow was not just strong and agile, he was powerful and a powerful tom cat is a sheer terror. Even a smallish tom cat is quite dangerous if aroused.

The young man tried to hit Mow and to grab his tail and pull it. In a flash Mow had turned and raked his needle sharp claws down the boys arm drawing blood. As the boy tried to push Mow away with his other hand Mow closed his teeth on it. Somehow the youth, desperate now to escape, had wrenched himself free and had run off crying in pain and shock, while Mow sauntered back to his favourite lookout place on the high branch of an oak tree near the park. Most cats can leap up to three times their length or more. They climb trees like lightning and they can twist and turn with amazing speed. No human could ever do what a cat does. In comparison we humans are very feeble and weedy.

Mow did not need humans but they needed him and were happy to provide him with all those little luxuries which cats think of as a sort of tribute humans pay to cats for the privilege of having them live with them. Mow's humans had the additional advantage that they had a big garden and a large patch of rhubarb under which Mow could hide and pounce out on the birds that came to peck the crumbs which the female human threw out for them.

Some of the antics Stephanie got up to with the humans amazed Mow. He watched from his branch and thought "how can an animal be so stupid, how can she be so lacking in all dignity?" Stephanie was running after a wooden ball which the male human threw for her. She kept it up and would have apparently gone on for ever if the human had not got tired. Mow shook his paws distastefully as he surveyed the sorry scene. Dogs had such a strange mentality and, to Mow's thinking, humans were just daft. On the other hand they served some useful purposes. Stephanie had come first to the house. She had been given to the humans by a friend and had settled in very happily. When Mow turned up the humans worried they might fight. Mow was nearly fully grown but still a bit kittenish. He enjoyed playing with the bull terrier's tail. She enjoyed

14

it too. He had been a stray and had turned up in the garden where he had caught and eaten a mouse. The female human had seen him and thought what a good idea it might be to have a cat to keep down vermin. As it turned out it was the one of the wisest decisions she had ever made.

They were eating fish and chips. They always did on a Thursday evening; the male bought them on his way home from work. The lady, who had been watching Mow took a lump of fish from her plate and opened the back door. Her husband called after her. "Shut the door there's a draught," and then yelled, "your food will get cold." The female took no notice but held out the fish so Mow could smell it. It was a scent more delicious than he had ever believed could exist. However he was a cat and had to make the woman realise that hers was the privilege to be giving food to a cat. So enticing was the smell of the fish that, having stepped carefully and suspiciously towards her, he then took the whole lump from her hand and wolfed it down.

A look of admiration came over the woman's face. "Oh isn't he sweet," she said. It was a remark which did not endear her to Mow, sweet? He did not think so. However, her next remark did make up for her lack of discernment somewhat. "Isn't he magnificent," she said more to herself than to her husband who had now come out to see what all the fuss was about. Now at this point in the story I must let you into a secret. It is not generally understood by humans that many of the more intelligent animals, and cats are among the most intelligent of all, can understand what we say and even, at times what we think.

15

The male human did not seem as impressed by Mow as the female. He knew that fate had decided that Mow would now adopt them. There was no getting away from the look on the female's face, she was totally smitten. However he had to have his little grumble. "He's a tom cat," said he glumly, "he'll keep us awake at night caterwauling and he'll get into fights with all the other tom cats and he'll populate the area with black and white kittens." (Mow was a black cat with a white bib, white socks on all his feet and a white patch on his nose.) He actually was quite cute but he preferred the word handsome, which was how all the lady cats saw him.

By this time the female human had picked up Mow and held him on one shoulder with his face close to her. Mow rubbed his neck against hers, not so much with affection but so as to mark her with his scent glands as a human that now belonged to him. He knew exactly what he was doing and his next ploy was to purr, a deep rumble from deep down in his chest. Neither of the humans could resist him, they were captured; hook line and sinker, while Stephanie looked on with amazement.

Most dogs annoyed Mow. Stephanie was placid and maternal and because she was a lady dog, and because Stafforshire dogs were once called 'nanny dogs because they are naturally fond of children. Mow felt protective of her. Not that she needed any protecting. She was a bull terrier and they are powerful dogs who are bred for fighting. No other dog could fight a bull terrier, they were stocky and exceptionally strong and even big dogs like German Shepherds did not have the aggression and the power of a bull terrier. In her way Stephanie felt protective of her humans and of Mow. Because Mow had not been quite full grown that she took to him in the way she did; she was maternal and protective. She was puzzled about a lot of things but whether Mow was a cat, a dog, or a catdog, puzzled her most of all.

It came about in this way. Bill, the male human, was called on one day by his Union Representative who came to tell him about a union meeting or a bowls club match, or something. He stood at the front door talking to Bill about this and that. Human males often do this, talking for hours, and then saying that it is the females who gossip endlessly. All the while they were talking the man's large black Labrador sat on the garden path behind him waiting to be taken for a walk in the park. Bill's union representative suddenly laughed and said. "I hear you have a cat. You'll have to watch out for this one he pointed over his shoulder with his thumb to the dog he's a devil for cats."

What he meant was that cats usually ran off when they saw the Labrador, or climbed a tree while the dog went into a frenzy of barking and the cat sat on a branch and watched the fun. Inside the house Stephanie could smell another dog and slowly began to take a mild interest. Was he from a rival pack, she wondered, or wouold he like to play. Behind the house, in the back garden a large black tom cat with white paws and a white front stalked under the fence and across the grass. He smelled dog. The dog did not smell anything except the more general smell of cat and dog which wafted from the house. He was not prepared for the apparition which came hissing and growling round the corner of the house like a demented steam engine bent on mayhem and destruction.

Mow's fur stood on end making him seem twice the size he was normally. His whiskers were laid back and his growl became a banshee howl of sheer malicious hatred. His tail lashed from side to side with anger at the temerity of this dog that dared to come, without his permission, onto his territory. The dog hardly had time to bare his teeth in warning before the typhoon of claws and teeth launched itself, like one of Zeus's lightning bolts, at his face. Mow was anger personified. His claws raked down each side of the dogs muzzle and, such was the impetus of the attack that the cat's rear legs swung forward so that their clawed feet dug into the dog's chest.

The Labrador howling in dismay and in pain and managed to free himself. He sprang away from the vengeful fury spitting with venomous anger and started to run flat out, helped on his way by more claws stabbing his rear and sharp white teeth burying themselves in his back leg. The cat pursued the Labrador up the road as neighbours dropped whatever it was they were doing to watch this amazing sight of a large dog being chased by an indignant tom cat.

"Cor! Blimey!" were the words that dropped from the mouth of the owner of the dog as his mouth dropped open in horror and dismay. He blinked in horror and surprise as his "devil with cats" disappeared round a bend in the road chased by the fury that was Mow the tom cat. Not the most profound of remarks but entirely appropriate given the circumstances.

"I never did like that Labrador," remarked the male human later on to the female. She replied, "I never did like his owner, nasty little man always trying to organize other people. I never could stand men who try to organize people, they're like little Hitlers." Mow did not know what a Hitler was let alone a little one. He did not much care; he was dozing curled up comfortably on the female human's lap while she and the male watched the television. He purred softly, content with life and with his humans; he thought to himself that he had them quite well trained.

The male human, who was also feeling a bit sleepy said, "I don't suppose we'll see much more of him." He felt much more well-disposed to cats in general and to Mow in particular after the earlier cat and dog confrontation.

Stephanie, stretched out by the radiator, also felt content. She had Mow worked out now entirely to her own limited satisfaction. The way he had vanquished the Labrador proved to her that Mow was actually the soul of a bull terrier in a feline body. His attack on the dog had proven it. Bull terriers she reasoned were bred to fight other dogs. Therefore, since Mow fought dogs he had to be a bull terrier in disguise. She fell asleep the puzzle solved.

MOW IN THE MORNING

(HOW MOW GOT HIS NAME)

By now you will have guessed that Mow got his name from the appreciative way he took the fish from the female human's hand. If so you would be quite wrong. It was nothing of the sort. When Mow took the fish he was not saying "thank you" cats do not say, "thank you," for what they consider is their right. Cats like Mow have a very high opinion of their own importance. Perhaps they are right. Perhaps not, who knows? The female human had, even before he had gulped the fish and swallowed it whole, decided that Mow should have a name. But what? It had to be something exotic; she certainly thought Mow was exotic, but not that exotic. He was not a Siamese or a Burmese cat, not even a Persian one. She thought maybe Jonah but rejected that as she tended to think of Jonah much as sailors do; a walking disaster.

Mow was regal and somewhat arrogant, a bit like a professional boxer or wrestler who gets himself crowned as king. It is difficult to think of a suitable name for a professional fighter who gets to be king. That would have been alright in the old days when kings were the top godfathers in the gangland protection racket that was Medieval Europe. She thought for a bit about Viking chieftains. Eric the Red, or Lief the Lucky but shortened to Lief or Eric they did not quite have the ring for the Viking chieftain sort of barbarian that Mow really was. Ragnar, she thought, then remembered that he was also known as 'hairy breeches'; again it did not sound quite right. Harald,

Sven, Canute, no! None of them suited. Maybe something Irish, Cuchulain, Brian Boru; no! Not Irish! She decided.

She spent a whole day going over names in her head. Roman Emperors seemed promising. Julius, Augustus, Tiberius, Vespasian, Titus, Claudius, Caligula, Nero. Claudius made her think twice but then she realized that she was connecting cats and claws with Claudius. That only seemed corny. Anyway, at least two of those others were stark raving bonkers and most of the rest were megalomaniacs, Vespasian had been a nice old man she thought and his military success gave him some affinity with the large cat who had taken up residence with them. She almost decided on Vespasian then thought that the male human would only laugh at her.

The only other thing she knew about emperors was that they spent a lot of time at the Colosseum giving the thumbs down to failed gladiators. She knew by this time that Mow (as he came to be known, as you shall find out soon) would have been down therein the arena giving the gladiators what for. The more she thought about Romans the more distasteful the subject became. The games were not your Saturday afternoon soccer match. She started going to the library to read books about cats. Cats in fiction tended to have daft names like Montmorency. Nobody, by any stretch of the imagination, could think of Mow as a Montmorency. She gave up on books and called him 'cat' for a few days.

It did not take long for Mow to get adventurous. Cats are naturally adventurous.

They say "curiosity killed the cat," but then 'they', whoever 'they' are, tend to say a lot of silly and stupid things. It is natural for a tom cat to patrol his territory each night. It was also natural, since tom cats are a bit like barbarian chieftains in that they like to steal territory from their neighbours. They are not like barbarian chieftains in that they do not have a gang of mounted, or seamanlike thugs to back them up.

Tom cats are loners who stalk the night. If other tom cats are bigger and more aggressive, then the territory of a tom cat may be very small, just their own back garden, and even that can be taken over by a bigger and more dominant male. Mow soon established himself, since he was the biggest, the most aggressive, and the most confident of tom cats, as the top cat for miles, literally.

For a few days he contented himself with establishing himself and ensuring that his milk and meals came at regular times so that he could fit in his other activities round mealtimes. At first he did not stay out all night but explored the house. The humans did not know but he explored thoroughly every inch, every nook and cranny. He even explored the loft, though how he got up there no one knows and Mow was certainly not going to tell them.

He was doing all this while they were asleep, of course. He soon learned where every mouse was, and where birds had made their nests. The mice were quick to pack their bags and leave, emigrating to other houses where the cats were either too well fed to hunt, or where there were no cats. Mice too had a keen sense of smell and the smell of cat pervaded the house now that a tom cat with keen hunting instincts was in residence.

To mark their territory cats will spray some areas. He sprayed the outside of the house and the trees bordering the park. He sprayed in the attic. It just shows how feeble humans are that they did not catch even a whiff of it, though to all other creatures it must have been overpowering'.
The female did give the odd sniff but thought it was something cooking next door. The lady next door considered herself an expert on Eastern cuisine and often strange and exotic cooking smells wafted round the area. Some people said the smells were 'weird' these people were the kind ones; others had more down to earth adjectives.

Having established his presence and his scent on everything inside and round the immediate outside, Mow decided it was high time he stayed out all night and extended his territory. A tom cat may cover a large area in a night and arrive back at daybreak with several victories over rival tom cats under his belt, and having sprayed every tree and gate post within as much as a square mile, or more.

With the sun coming up Mow returned to his house and to his humans. He had had fights with two rival toms and had, within seconds established that he was the boss cat. Several lady cats had been flattered to have the attentions of such a handsome and powerful young male. All in all it had been a good night and he expected his humans to be there to greet him on his return. It ought to have been a, "see the conquering hero comes" return, but it wasn't. The sun was shining brightly but the curtains were still drawn and his humans were still asleep. It was something after five and high time for any self-respecting cat to be washing himself carefully all over before settling down for a day of sleeping and eating.

The humans, unimaginative creatures that they were, seemed to think that cats ate at the same time as they did. To a healthy cat this is ridiculous. They are naturally opportunistic. Cats eat whenever they can. If humans give them milk in the morning, chicken at noon and fish in the early evening that is O.K. by them. It does not mean that they ought not to go out to snaffle other cats' dinners that have been left outside back doors for them. Nor does it mean they will not tuck into the contents of some badly situated black bin bag.

Mow soon got into the habit of turning up his aristocratic nose (note, all cats are aristocratic) at his own dinner and going off to see what he could beg, borrow, filch or steal before coming back and deigning to eat what the humans had put out for him. It took them nearly a year, dim-witted things that they were, to cotton on to this. By which time it was too late to change so they still went on putting out choice bits of chicken for him which he sniffed at before going off for a spot of larceny. In this way he got them to remember who was boss and who were the servants. That particular morning he sat on the back doorstep. He waited but soon became impatient. When tom cats get impatient they let you know. They also let the neighbours know and anyone else, like postmen or paper boys or tramps as well.

You cannot possibly imagine the range of meaning a cat can put into a simple word like 'mow'. You cannot imagine, of course you can't, if you are reading this you are human and therefore slow, dull, and intellectually challenged; compared with cats, that is. You cannot possibly imagine or conceive how loudly a big cat can complain. Mow complained, long and hard. It was a 'mow' that said, loudly and demanding." Get out of bed, you lazy good for nothing humans. Get my milk. The sun is up and I need, I demand, my milk! NOW!"

There was silence for five minutes or just less then the cry was taken up again. First it was demanding then it changed to a pleading, wheedling sort of tone, saying. "I am a poor betrayed and neglected feline. My humans have abandoned me. Will someone please let me in before I die of cold and starvation." There is nothing like a spot of blackmail followed up, of course with the demands so that the cat does not lose face.

The plaintive note gradually changed to a fiercer one, saying. "LET ME IN AT ONCE! GIVE ME MY MILK. I WANT IT NOW! I DEMAND MY RIGHTS! NOW! HOW DARE YOU NEGLECT ME LIKE THIS. HOW DARE YOU SHUT ME OUT WHEN I HAVE DONE SO MUCH FOR YOU."

In reality cats do nothing for their besotted hosts but they have this skill of the accomplished con artist that they can make themselves at home in your house, eat your food, sleep on your bed and then make you believe they are doing you a tremendous favour just by living with you and eating your food.

Next came the ultimatum. "LET ME IN OR I SHALL DISOWN YOU BOTH LET ME IN OR I WILL FIND ANOTHER HOUSE AND HUMANS WHO APPRECIATE A CAT OF MY DISTINCTION. LISTEN TO ME, I MEAN IT!"

This was followed by a repeat of all this all over again. Being humans they did not understand the finer points but began to get the gist of it. It was a bit like that song children sing to get adults really upset. "I know a song that will drive you insane, drive you insane, drive you insane." After this has been sung about fifty times over, normal adults are climbing screaming up the wall. Metaphorically speaking that is, cats they are not, so cannot really climb walls, but you know what I mean.

"For heaven's sake," grumbled the male human, "it's the crack of dawn."

"It's the cat,' said his wife. "Why don't you let him in?"

"He's your cat," he argued in a sleepy and annoyed voice. "He's your cat as well."

"Not at this time in the morning he isn't."

"He'll wake the neighbours."

"He's our cat so let him in, he'll wake the whole town."

"He already has I should imagine."

"Then let him in for heaven's sake."

"If you had any consideration you'd let him in."

Having said that, she put the pillow over her head and tried to go back to sleep; it was impossible and they were now both wide awake so they got up. The male human was muttering about vets and having him, 'seen to'. The female human was indignant and said it would be both cruel and expensive. By this time he were fumbling with the key to the back door. He opened it and Mow stalked in

If you think he had been idle, simply sitting there complaining and kicking up the most awful row you would be terribly wrong. The most intelligent cats always think. They plan and they weigh up possible courses of action with a view to the best advantage for themselves. Mow had at first decided to be angry, and, as soon as they had opened up to stalk off and sulk up the oak tree, going to sleep on his favourite branch. He quickly realized that this would deprive him of his morning milk and could even alienate the male human who was known to 'fly off the handle' as humans put it. He knew he had to work on the male as well as keeping the female in her cat-besotted state.

As soon as the door was open he ran in as if he had been rescued after being kidnapped by cat-nappers. He leaped over the threshold with a cry of joy. It was "Mow" with a sort of "rrrp" at the end. "A delightful little chirrup," as the female human put it later on to one of her cat loving cronies. He rubbed his head against her ankles purring loudly and then turned his attention to the male and rubbed his ankles too with lots of purring as well.

The man appeared to be unimpressed but secretly he was gratified. "Oh he's so sweet," said the female and she picked him up to stroke him. "He's so pleased to see us," she cooed.

Still grumpy though a bit pleased that Mow had noticed him, he said, "He's pleased at the prospect of getting his morning milk which you seem to have made a habit of."

"Huh!" sniffed his wife, "who gave him milk before getting off to work two days last week?"

"That was only because you were having a lie in," answered the male human huffily.

All this time the fridge was being opened, a carton taken out and milk was poured into the dish which they all had come to agree was Mow's own special private property.

Mow lapped up his milk with a confident air. He was sure that they would not leave him out any more. In this he somewhat miscalculated and reproached himself for a serious lack of judgment, later on. Though it was gratifying to hear the female human say, "I think he really loves us you know."

"Cupboard love," answered her husband cynically, he knows we feed him, not just stuff out of tins either, but best bits of chicken and fish, he'll eat us out of house and home soon."

"He loves us, doesn't oo catikins?" said the wife in a daft voice with the sort of tone that said that was final.

In spite of the female telling her husband not to be a grouch, Mow decided he had a lot of work to do to make sure the male human completely accepted him. He realised too that he would have his work cut out. This came home to him more forcefully when the saw the male human nailing bits of wood to an old box and then putting it outside the back door and putting a plastic cover over the top of it, leaving a gap in the front. "Catikins!" Scoffed the male human, "I'll give him Catikins."

That afternoon, after the male had come in from work, the female human asked again. "What do you think we should call him?" Without a moment's hesitation the man answered, "'Mow'! He said it often enough this morning." "What!" Said the female human, "That isn't a name." "Oh! Yes it is!" answered the male. Just watch, listen and learn. I have cat psychology all worked out. In that, of course, he was seriously mistaken.

Mow looked up suspiciously as the male human squatted on the floor near him. The male tried to look him directly in the eye but had to blink for no human can outstare a cat. "What's your name then?" he asked looking again at Mow.

Mow's reply was rather rude, if you could understand feline you would know that. He said, "On yer bike, don't play silly games with me!" It came out to the dull hearing and the duller understanding of the humans as "Mow". And that is how he got his name. But neither had he quite finished his campaign to worm his way into the male human's affections as you shall see.

CAT AND DOG SHOW

"And as I was saying." Stephanie tried to look important and drew herself up to
her full height, taking in a deep breath ready to go on with her fantastic revelation. Mow spoiled it all by breaking in on her big moment. "I bet you want to tell me you heard the humans talking about us." He yawned and closed his eyes to make it look as if he was going to sleep. Stephanie looked hurt.

"Don't you want to know what they were saying?" she asked a little irritably.

Mow opened one eye. "If I must," he said. "If it's human talk it can't be very important." He made as if to settle down to sleep again. He did really want to hear but he did not want to make Stephanie feel important. He was a cat and you know how difficult cats are. They never do what you want them to do, and they think themselves to be superior to all other animals, which in a way they are.

Stephanie felt deflated but she struggled on. She had badly wanted to tell her news and even now she felt that Mow would be surprised and pleased. How little she knew about cats. Stephanie admired Mow. She thought he was really a bull terrier in a feline body. Ever since he had chased the Labrador up the street she was convinced of this. The news she had to tell seemed to her tremendously exciting. Just because it was exciting to her as a dog, she could not understand why Mow was often less than enthusiastic about these things.

Bull Terriers are not the brightest spark in the box of fireworks but even they can get the feeling someone is mocking them. However she did at least know that she could never get one over on Mow, so she did not try. "Well do you want to hear or don't you," Stephanie demanded.

"I'm all ears," replied Mow, his voice positively dripping with sarcasm, which was completely lost on Stephanie. She wondered, for a moment, how he could be all ears, but gave up the thought knowing that it was something peculiar to cats that they got a bit mixed up. His ears did prick up a little which was encouraging after the slow start. She took another deep breath and began her story. "Well!" She commenced, "they were talking as they often do in the kitchen. She said to him that the village carnival was coming up in a few days time."

Mow blinked lazily. "So!" He said, "what has that got to do with us?" He was pretending to be lazy but in fact she had most of his attention by this time. Human activities were all very well but they were usually noisy or smelly. Though, on the other hand, some of the smells were often food smells which was not a bad thing for an opportunistic cat, or for that matter a dog. "I was just coming to that," said Stephanie huffily.

"Oh! Sorry!" said Mow, "Do go on.""Thank you," she said, with an attempt at sarcasm. "Anyway," she went on, "she, the female one, said that they were having a cat and dog show." If Stephanie expected a response she was disappointed. Mow merely looked a little startled and a tiny bit worried. Stephanie struggled on. "There's to be a children's pet show as well, all in a big marquee and she, the human female, said she would like to enter us in the cat and dog shows

." She paused and then exclaimed, "isn't that exciting? We can't help but win, you the cat show and me the dog show." Mow said nothing. He was paralysed with shock and horror. His blood seemed to run cold. The idea, the indignity, made his whiskers shiver and his tail to go all crinkly with unanswered questions. His sense of self preservation and the secretiveness natural to all cats, made him think quickly and carefully before he said anything. Best to change the subject, he thought.

"Mm!" he said, "it is, of course a foregone conclusion that such handsome and intelligent animals as we are would win any competition of the sort, indeed any competition at all." He stopped to choose his words carefully, then went on. "However humans, even those who claim to understand us, which they cannot for a moment do, with their limited intelligence, they cannot possibly know enough to judge the merits of animals. No! It is certain that they will choose some fat lazy Persian cat full of fish and cream, or, in your case something like that miniature poodle at the hairdressers, or that spaniel over the road." He shook his head sadly. "We must admit it," he said, "Humans are stupid and utterly lacking in good taste and discernment."

Stephanie had to agree. She thought of the Spaniel over the road. "I could always bite their legs off," she said wistfully, her aggressive bull terrier nature coming to the fore at the thought of the shame of only getting a 'Highly Commended' instead of the first prize.

Mow thought very carefully again. He was about to suggest that they both absconded for a few days but he stopped as he realized that dogs did not easily manage to be secretive nor to hide properly. If the humans came after them she was all too likely to leap out of their hiding place barking and wagging her tail at the pleasure of seeing them again. Even if she did get away she was not really a hunting dog and she had no idea of scrounging in dustbins for food. Indeed she considered it rather disgusting. That was another thing she did not understand. After all food was food wherever it was and to a cat that was all that mattered.

He thought about trying to hunt with a dog to accompany him. Dogs thought of hunting as running after something and barking like mad. They had no idea of slinking stealthily and silently, like a shadow, through the bushes and leaping out on an unsuspecting mouse or bird. No it would be out of the question.

Stephanie was looking puzzled so Mow said kindly to her. "Don't worry; we know our value even if we are not truly appreciated by humans in general. It's something we have to live with. All the truly great animals have been like that, never appreciated by their own generation nor by the humans."

Stephanie looked a little less despondent. "Is that so she asked?"

"Of course, of course," said Mow reassuringly, "it is always the case."

She still felt a little bit puzzled but assumed, in her innocence, that Mow would be right. She was about to say something but while she was thinking what it was she forgot it. Just at that moment the humans came into the room. The male human was still not sure about the idea, but the female one was full of enthusiasm. "We will have to give Stephanie a bath," she was saying, "and put nice ribbons round their necks. They will look really sweet."

You can tell by this how besotted the female human was with her own ideas and with the two animals she considered to be her pets. The male human shook his head. He knew that once she got an idea into her head that was it, but he did not have to like it and what he did was under protest. "That cat," he announced, looking in Mow's direction, "is not going to take kindly to ribbon round his neck. Nor," he went on, "can I see him sitting quietly while the Mayoress totters round on those awful high heels of hers and strokes all the cats and dogs.

Anyway what if that big ginger Tom is there as well? That cat's owner is a silly old biddy she's bound to put him into the show." Mow's reaction to all this was a sort of "yuck!" He felt sick and angry at the same time. It confirmed all that he had guessed. There would be no ribbon round his neck that was for certain. Even if they could catch him he would fight and scratch until they let him go. The very idea made him feel seriously ill. As for Ginger Tom, just let him be anywhere near Mow and the fur would fly, that was for sure.

The male human did not fancy having to catch Mow and put him into a cat box.

He would fight and scratch and bite and the teeth of a full grown tom cat can be pretty formidable, he knew. Any way, he thought to himself, I can't say I blame the cat, if I was him I would not want to be part of a cat show. He thought again. What if pets put humans in human shows, would he be pleased to be put into a human cage and displayed and fussed over with ribbon round his neck? In spite of everything he had said about Mow the male human was clearly a lot more feline aware than his wife and more than the two animals had given him credit for.

Later, Mow asked Stephanie when this show was to be. "A couple of weeks, I think," she answered vaguely. "You don't really like the idea, do you?" she said. This showed that she was capable of a lot more intelligent thinking than Mow had credited her with.

"To be honest," admitted Mow, "not at all. You enjoy it if you want to but don't get your hopes up, there'll be some stupid, over the top poodle or spaniel, with its fur all curled and perfumed and some cretinous human judge will give them the prize. An honest guard dog like yourself with twice their strength and fitness does not stand a chance. This is not about the merits of animals but about human politics. They've got elections coming up and the Mayoress wants to make herself popular and the owners of that awful poodle have a lot of influence in the townswomen's guild and the lodge."

Stephanie looked sad and hurt but Mow went on. "Please don't get upset. I know, and our humans know that you are a better dog by far than any other in the whole town. You know perfectly well that you could make mincemeat of that poodle and the spaniel as well and then crunch up their bones. But then you also know that humans are lacking in all the finer points of discernment. It is something we animals have to live with."

Stephanie felt quite moved to hear Mow's good opinion of her. She knew that he was clever and cunning and cynical and to hear such things was quite unexpected. For his part Mow really did like Stephanie and could almost feel it in his heart to forgive her for being a dog. He also knew that she could never be anything like a cat so he accepted her as she was, as she accepted and liked him.

After that Mow seemed to go to sleep until it was getting dark and he decided to go out. He sat by the back door and demanded, loudly, to be let out, until the male human got up from his chair and grumbling opened the door for him. Mow slunk off into the night a plan already forming in his active and agile mind. He went exploring.

It is surprising what information a cat can glean after all humans have gone to bed. There were posters all over the place. He could not read them, of course, but their very presence meant that something was on. There were chains of lights and bunting and flags. All this confirmed what Stephanie had said. He waited for the big day to draw near. He had two things on his mind. The first was to sense when the cat and dog show was actually going to happen. The second was to lull his humans into a false sense of security. He had to let them think he was getting fat and lazy and would be easily caught and put in a cat basket for transport to the marquee.

The town carnival was to be celebrated with sports for the children and young adults, there were games arranged for the children and the town band was to play. There was a travelling fair which set up in a field next to the one where the sports were to be held. A big marquee was set up and several smaller marquees for various activities including lunch for the VIP's which, as you know is for those humans who have somehow managed to convince themselves that they are more important than all the other humans.

Mow considered all the dressing up and posturing that humans did as rather foolish. For him life was just a matter of hunting, keeping the humans happy and in a biddable frame of mind, putting other tom cats in their proper places and keeping his lady-cat friends happy. The activity of dealing with rivals gave him endless satisfaction and the admiration of all the lady cats in the area. There was just one fly in the ointment of his contentment and that was Ginger Tom, who was not yet persuaded that Mow was the dominant male cat in the area. Mow determined at their next meeting he would be fully persuaded, even if it did cost Mow a torn ear.

From his favourite tree branch Mow watched the goings on at the other side of the park. The fair interested him. What a lot of fuss humans made about perfectly useless things, he thought to himself. A fair, as far as he was concerned, was a lot of noise, loud music, or what passed for music;

and lots of flashing lights. It was enough to turn a cat's stomach.

When they had discussed it earlier in the day Stephanie had agreed, which showed that she was getting a lot more sensible and aware. Perhaps, he thought, his influence was bearing fruit, albeit rather slowly.

Though fairs, generally, were an anathema to Mow, this one, he thought might well serve a useful purpose. The next day was to be the cat and dog and pet show in the big marquee. Mow stayed in his tree, hidden among the leaves. "You had better get that cat in," the woman reminded her long-suffering husband. "He will try to get away or the fair noise will frighten him, or something, and he will not be there when we want him for the show." "How right you are lady," said Mow to himself. No amount of shouting brought any response.

The man looked up into the tree but could not see Mow. Even had he been there the human would not have been able to see him. But he was not there and that was why the man shouted and pleaded in vain. At least he had to be seen to be doing something in order to please the female human. As soon as the door had opened Mow had slipped quietly down the trunk on the other side from the house and had crept off into the long grass at the edge of the park.

Once securely hidden he watched the crowds flocking to the fair and then carefully slid through the grass and the bushes to make sure he knew where everything was. He smiled to himself as only cats can smile to themselves. He thought of Stephanie being bathed and combed and decked out with a ribbon on her collar. "Not on your nelly," he said to himself, "you don't catch Mow making a fool of himself like that."

"He's not had his tea!" the woman was saying anxiously. "Don't be daft!" was her husband's unsympathetic reply, "he'll be off robbing some other cat of its dinner or foraging in dustbins or eating left over chips by the fish and chip shop. I've seen him hanging about there before." "Don't be disgusting," she snapped back. "Mow is too, er too, er fastidious and respectable" she said, "he would not dream of eating left overs."

"Wouldn't he just," thought her husband, but he did not say it. This just goes to show how when anthropomorphism rules humans lose all their boasted intelligence and become not just naïve but quite daft. Mow was at that moment behind the burger van in the shadows eating some suspicious looking and smelling sausages that had been discarded as not quite fit for human consumption. Indeed he also had a choice of half eaten burgers which he also appreciated.

After exploring the carnival site he went off through the industrial estate and visited some of the lady cats who lived there in the houses beyond the factory units. They spent the night singing to each other; Mow being rather proud of his singing voice. The lady cats were also very impressed and, what with the noise of the fair the neighbours were nearly driven mad. Lack of sleep caused several family quarrels the next day. One woman complained to her neighbor. "If it wasn't the shouting an' the screaming an' the loud music of the fair, it was cats a caterwauling', an' screechin'. You never 'eard such a noise, couldn't get a wink of sleep and my ole man 'as gone down to the pub an' 'e promised to take us all to the carnival."

So said one lady resident to her neighbor. The neighbor shook her head and agreed that the row from the fair was bad enough, but that the cats sounded like a whole host of banshees being tortured to death. They agreed that they had been deprived of sleep and that the council ought to do something about it. Just what that should be they were less certain about.

As for Mow he had had a very enjoyable night and was now determined to find somewhere to sleep until the carnival was safely over. He thought of returning to his tree but decided that might be a little too close to his humans. Instead he set off once more to explore the marquees and the burger van. The sausages had tasted quite good the night before. He thought how considerate some humans could be to leave food out for him. Cats always think that the world revolves around them so any happy chances like left over burgers and sausages were meant to be intended for them to their way of thinking.

All this was part of Mow's cunning plan. After much thought and planning, he had decided that he would hide near the carnival. Discarded burgers and slightly off sausages had been a bonus. He made his way stealthily to the far side of the showground which was in the municipal park. He was about to settle for a sleep when he heard movements and, from the road entrance to the park had heard some vehicles arriving.

A lesser cat might have fled off home. Mow did not. Mow was not a lesser cat. Mow was top cat and he dared any human or any dog, except for Stephanie to challenge him. He was full grown and he was big and heavy. It took an effort on the part of his male human to pick him up. Since he was also all muscle and could climb and jump and run there was no human on earth who could hold him if he did not want to be held.

Slowly, senses alert, he took a walk, his tail erect in the air, along the side of the marquee. Curiosity is an important part of a cat's mental make-up. He could sleep in the trees but they were too open and the ground was a little too exposed. He wanted somewhere secluded where he would be hidden. There were human smells aplenty. There were also some faint animal aromas, among them a distinct smell of rabbit and guinea pig. Both these were intriguing; especially as Mow knew they were also delicious. He had once caught a rabbit and had eaten it raw. That was before he had adopted his humans and let them have the privilege of feeding him.

Old Mrs. Gumbles at the Post Office never knew what had happened to her guinea pig. Somehow it seemed to have opened its cage and got out. Only Mow knew what had really happened and he was not going to tell anyone. He was looking forward to the next tasty meal of guinea pig.

There was a point where the brailing at the bottom of the marquee wall had come undone. Maybe the peg had been put in badly. Maybe it was just inefficiency on the part of the workmen, which in the light of later events seems to have been much more likely. But there it was; whatever the cause it was Mow's opportunity, and he took it.

Mow squeezed through the gap and surveyed the interior. Tables covered in soft material lined each side of the large tent and at one end. There was also a double row in the middle. Most of the tables were empty but there were bits and pieces lying about and at one end there was a role of the material which humans call 'green baize' left by itself on a spare table. Mow, in one fluid motion, leapt from the floor onto the material and began to circle round and to knead the soft stuff with his claws. It was just the sort of material to make a cat comfortable he decided.

Since there were seemed to be no humans present he concluded he would be undisturbed for some hours yet. How thoughtful of the humans to leave it all for him he decided. He woke after a couple of hours with the sun streaming through a gap that had mysteriously appeared in one of the tent walls. A car, then another one, drew up outside and human voices could be heard. Mow raised his head, fully awake but reluctant to leave his luxurious little nest. He would wait, he decided, and see what would happen.

What happened was a group of women carrying boxes and bags which they took to the far end away from where Mow was ensconced. "Better not go opening tins yet," said a voice. "Drat, I've already begun," replied another. The first voice, in a weary tone, explained. "It's only in case any of the poor little kitties and doggies get hungry. You know how some owners do not feed their animals before a show.

Horror struck into Mow's consciousness. He was in the last place he had intended to be; he was, horror of horrors, in the marquee of the cat and dog show. He gathered his legs beneath him ready to spring for the opening in the wall of the tent. He was ready to spring when something else, gently then with increasing attraction and firmness, intruded into his senses. Mow breathed deeply and the scent of something delicious wafted toward him. Mow stopped, he listened and he sniffed the air. There was something. It was tantalizing and fragrant, to a cat that is. It became stronger and it was a distinct smell of fish.

Mow followed his nose. It was from the other end of the marquee that the aroma of fish came to him on the early morning breeze. The woman had been opening a tin of some sort of fish. It was not tuna, it could have been pilchards, he was not sure. He certainly had no intention of making a dash for freedom when there were tins of fish being opened. He simply had to investigate. He did not think that the humans at the far end stood any chance at all of stopping him if he made a dash for the exit.

Carefully and with dignity he stalked along the table on which he had been sleeping. He stopped his eyes fixed on the tray of tins with one half open, and a lady dithering with it in her hand wondering what to do with it now she had begun to open it. Mow was quite sure he knew what she ought to do. It was a matter of transference. That is to transfer the fish from inside the tin to the inside of Mow in the shortest possible time and with the least possible fuss.

He sat on the table and he looked at her and he looked at the fish. It was as if the lady could feel the eyes boring into her back. She turned, and as she did so the man who had complained about the tins of fish and of dog food also turned. "Wherever did that dratted cat come from?" he demanded of the world in general. That 'dratted cat' was not impressed by the man's tone and glared at him before turning back to the lady with the tin and giving her the 'poor, neglected hungry feline' look. "Oh!" exclaimed the lady, "isn't he a gorgeous cat?" Clearly a human of intelligence thought Mow and he gave her a "mow" which said much the same sort of thing as the look had been intended to convey.

He continued to stare at the fish and, to emphasize the point, he licked his lips a couple of times. The lady who was about as clueless as any human can get, got the point finally. Anyway she had had this vision of herself dishing out goodies to grateful pussy-cats, not realizing that a cat show was not a cat party. She had a lot to learn about cats. She was certainly no match for the tom cat who was approaching her delicately with his most winning and appealing expression pasted on over the cynicism and greed which was his habitual and normal state.

The man was about to say something. He did manage another "dratted cat" but got a withering stare from the woman. She finished opening the tin and tried to tip out just one fish. She had intended that all the dear little kitties should share equally and should all go away happy, having had a nice snack of fish. Mow, of course, was of a different mind. The contents of the tin emptied themselves with a rush onto a plate which the woman had put on the table.

Before anyone could move, or the woman put some of the fish back, Mow was on it gulping fish down himself as fast as he could. It is amazing how a comparatively small animal like a cat can put away enough fish to make a full grown human feel it was too much. The woman stood and stared. She really was naive. Large, aggressive and hungry tom cats she did not, and never would, understand. Most humans are slow on the uptake. This one was positively brought to a standstill. She could not believe it. It was more like one of those conjuring tricks performed by stage magicians. "For my next trick ladies and gentlemen, I will make this tin of fish disappear in seconds, never to be seen by human eyes again."

Mow looked up, licked his lips, and coolly turned his back on his benefactor. He sat regally and washed himself carefully all over. He then sauntered back to where he had been sleeping where, after a few circles of his body to get comfortable, he settled down and was soon blissfully asleep again.

"Did you see that" breathed the woman. "You've just made his day," said the man. "That animal is not a pussy cat; it is a full grown tom cat. If you can imagine a mature male tiger getting into a field full of sheep that is what you have done for him." "He was magnificent," breathed the woman, "he positively gulped the fish down, a whole tinful. How did he do it?"

The man laughed, "easily, is the answer to that," he said still laughing. "Your face was a picture. Anyone would think you expected your average moggy or old lady's pet pussy cat. Anyone would think you have never seen a full grown male cat. They are about as civilized as Attila the Hun and about as cunning and as cynical as Machiavelli."

"He was magnificent," breathed the woman with a stunned and besotted expression on her face, something like a fish after it has been landed by a fisherman. Which just goes to show again how daft some humans can get. No wonder they are a pushover for Hitlers, Stalins and other assorted conmen. And for Mow, of course.

An hour later Mow was awoken by further activity and more voices. The lady who had given him the fish, still with that admiringly besotted expression on her face was talking to another woman. They were looking in Mow's direction and began to move towards him. He yawned, it was still sleeping time and the increasing bustle and conversation was disturbing him. He was not pleased. Humans should have more consideration, he thought.

"And you should have seen him, just as if he owned the place and we were all there to serve him." The fish lady was telling her story to the other woman. She, for her part was a large lady who had an air of importance about her. This was especially noticeable since all the other humans tended to treat her with respect. She had bleached hair and looked very well fed herself. She wore a smart black suit and her jewellery was real, as were her leather shoes, gloves and handbag. She was clearly worth a bob or two.

She wore a badge which said "Carnival Committee. Chair Person"

Even had he been able to read Mow would not have known what a chair person was though he tended to think of himself as that sort of animal, whether it was sleeping on chairs, especially the favourite chairs of certain humans or as one who dominated the proceedings; any proceedings, anywhere at any time. However Mow did understand dominance and power. This lady was clearly a dominant female and, as such, presented a challenge to Mow which he could not resist. There was also about her a distinct smell of cat, of Tom Cat, which demanded an immediate and thorough investigation.

He sat up, and then slid from the table to the ground in one lithe movement. With dignity, to show he was conferring a favour, he stalked towards the dominant human female and rubbed himself against her legs with enough of a purr to please the woman but not enough to suggest, for one moment that he was begging for favours. Perish the thought.

"I think he must be even bigger than my tom cat," said the important lady in admiration. Both the ladies were busy stroking and fussing over Mow. He loved it. It was, of course, his right that he should be so fussed over and admired, and he accepted their homage with all the dignity he possessed.

They were interrupted by the entry of a couple of workmen. The ladies both straitened up and the Chair Person asked, imperiously. "Are you the men who have come to put those ropes straight? It looks dangerous to me." The men in overalls knew on which side their bread was buttered. The important lady was not only the Chair Person of the Carnival Committee but chair of a whole variety of other committees in the Borough and a prominent member of the Borough Council. In particular she was Chair Person of the Entertainments Committee which was the branch of the Council for whom they worked. "Yes Mam!" said the older of the two.

The younger one just gawped, with his mouth wide open, until the older one told him to close his mouth and to stop looking as if he was trying to catch flies in it. He explained, respectfully. "We made it secure last night but we're just now tidying up. We had to clean up after the contractors in the VIP tent, they left a mess."

None of this was actually true but it gave the Chair Person the impression that they had been hard at work since early that morning. They had not. Indeed they had got up late and had only just arrived for work. The older man had had one or two jars too many, the night before, and had overslept. The younger one was gormless anyway and always overslept unless his mate telephoned to wake him. Because of his hangover he had forgotten and everything was a bit of a rush with neither of them feeling too well and neither of them having been fortified with their usual full English breakfast.

They commenced work while the two ladies continued to fuss over Mow and other people arrived with an assortment of boxes and cages. Mow began to feel it was time to think of making his escape but he had to balance that with the possibility that these two ladies might well think of opening another tin of fish. It would never do for him to dismiss that gourmet possibility. As you will have guessed, cats will do anything for food, especially if they are healthy and active tom cats, like Mow.

"Pull it tight!" The older workman was having trouble with his mate. That the mate was slow on the uptake was something of an understatement. When it came to uptake, he was usually on the down take. "No not that one, you nelly! That one there!"

The youth seemed to get the idea while his older workfellow muttered about what his old Chief Bo'sun's mate would have said about such ineptitude. It cannot be put down here since most of it, apparently, was in a language known only to seafaring men, of which select company the older man had once been.

While they were wrestling with the ropes which secured the beam which held up the canvas roof of the tent, a little man entered staggering under the weight of a large cage with a very disgruntled ginger cat in it. "Geraldine!" said the man in an aggrieved tone, "where do I put this wretched cat, he's been no end of trouble, and he's scratched my arm and bitten my thumb, twice," he added.

The Chair Lady waved her husband, for that was who the little man was, to a place on a table near the middle of the marquee. "Just put him there for a bit," she commanded and her longsuffering husband hurried to obey and to get rid of the "wretched cat". That was when everything started to go wrong. If anything could fall over it did so. If anything could unravel it did so. If anyone could trip, fall over, or bump into someone else they did so. Of course there had to be a reason for it all. There had to be a cause. People argued over causes and reasons for a long time afterwards.

The consequences also were out of all proportion to the relatively minor mishaps which had set everything in motion. Half the council threatened to resign. There were acrimonious scenes in the council chamber over whether there was ever to be another Carnival. People wrote to the papers over what a disaster it had all been. Thieves broke into the Mayor's parlour and stole the silverware and some very valuable pieces of civic property including some paintings by a semi-famous local artist. This may not have been connected to the disaster at the Carnival but people said it was a sign of the general inefficiency of the existing council and its Chair of the Entertainment Committee in particular.

Either her husband had forgotten to put on the catch to the cage into which he had managed to force Mow's arch rival the Ginger Tom, or it had come loose by itself. "There you are Tiger," he muttered under his breath. Just you wait here until her ladyship decides what she wants to do with you. He glared at his wife's cat with a look which suggested what he would like to do with the pair of them if he had his way. Tiger, the ginger tom, glared back, he reciprocated his human's husband's dislike with interest and an intensity which the man would have found impossible to imagine. At the same time he noticed that the cage door was loose.

Cats are ever opportunistic. He was through it in a flash. Before the human female's husband had time to catch his breath Tiger had made his escape and was even more determined that he would never again suffer the indignity of being put into a cage and transported to a cat and dog show. He leaped down from the table and…came face to face with Mow, his arch rival and sworn enemy.

For a couple of seconds only there was an eerie silence and then, like an orchestra tuning up, there came a sound so horrible, so full of malice and hatred that every person in that marquee, afterwards swore that it really made their flesh creep. They went cold and came out in gooseflesh. Strong men went weak at the knees and at least one old lady, who had been lifting her safely neutered and perfectly house-trained kitty onto the show table, fainted. The cat, terrified, slipped out of her grasp and made for the gap in the tent wall as fast as its legs could carry it.

The ghastly noise was a prelude to a sudden frenzy of spitting, scratching, swearing, feline aggression and hatred. One moment the two giant toms had been nose to nose making the most hideous and unearthly wailing and then there was just this whirlwind, this frenzy, this rapidly revolving ball of venom and vituperation. The younger of the two workmen was still clinging to the pieces of rope. His mate quickly let go and tried to grab the cats. Without a pause in the fight both big cats bit the man on his hand and one of them raked his claws down the man's arm. He was lucky it was not his face.

Seeing his mate letting go of the rope and howling with anger and pain the younger man also let go and went to see what the matter was. As people often say, "well! Things can only get worse," so the situation in the cat and dog marquee. With the rope now loose the beam holding the canvas roof up slid down the two big poles which held the whole tent up. Fortunately it only gave the important lady's husband a glancing blow before wedging itself against one of the uprights.

The lady chair person afterwards said it served him right for letting Tiger out of his cage. He said, but not in her hearing, it was all her fault for not organizing things properly and seeing that council workmen were up to their job. He claimed that council employees were, by and large, a gang of useless layabouts about as effective as a garden gnome in a fishing contest. However he was also careful to say that only in neutral hearing. It did get to the local paper though, which called for an investigation of certain councillors and the expenses they claimed for serving the Borough.

By this time everything was in a state of chaos. Cats and dogs still arriving began to get excited and to run round in circles. Bewildered owners of pets ran round like the proverbial headless chickens looking for their animals. Some of the animals were racing home in terror. Others were busy taking advantage of the situation and had got into the children's pets tent. It was mayhem, literally. A couple of lurchers swiftly killed four of the rabbits and carried the dead bodies off in triumph to their owners.

At least one civil court case arose from this quite understandably disastrous event. Various other small animals came to an early demise and some of these were eaten by the dogs and cats who had caused that demise. Two snakes, quite harmless ones actually, but one was a python and did not look harmless, frightened small children and any adult of a nervous disposition. The python actually had quite a good time since several pet rats had been among the exhibits.

Two old army veterans sat on a bench enjoying it all and one said to the other. "Never seen such a scattering match since Dunkirk, at least the Germans are not shooting at us here."

Meanwhile two large tom cats had fought each other to a standstill. Both were bleeding from numerous cuts and scratches and both would carry torn ears to the grave. By mutual consent they agreed to a rest between rounds agreeing to carry on the contest at some future date to be decided when one or the other invaded his rival's territory.

They stalked off. They were tired but content. They only agreed on one thing other than the truce, and that was that all humans were incorrigibly stupid, unpredictable and brainless. When his humans returned from the Carnival, having had a good time together on the bumper cars and the Vampire ride, they found Mow asleep in his box. At least, they thought he was asleep but he watched them with one of his eyes and listened for the clatter of dishes to remind him that it was tea time and in an hour or so adventure would be beckoning in the great outdoors.

"What has he done to his ears?" Gasped the female human, "and he's got blood on his nose!" "Seems like he's been fighting," answered her husband. "Another tom I expect to decide which one can get at all the female cats. There's be a plague of black and white kittens before we know where we are," he laughed.

MOW AND THE BURGLAR

"Yer!" the shifty looking character was enjoying the admiring audience who were listening to him boasting about his exploits. "Yer!" he said again, not quite sure how to go on. He was well away and a small but insistent voice was warning him not to go blabbing. It was too much for him however. The three younger men sitting on bar stools next to him round the curve of the bar seemed to be drinking in his every word almost as fast as he was drinking mouthfuls from his pint on the bar before him.

"Go on then Lofts," one of his cronies encouraged him with a wink at his mates, "tell us 'ow you an' Big Ernie done that 'ouse in Sackville Street. The one yer said that was a pushover."

The would-be king of crime put on a knowing expression and put a forefinger to the side of his nose. "I ain't sayin' too much, Big Ernie knew someone an' that someone got us in."

He stopped and took a gulp at his pint. Before he knew it another one appeared on the bar near his hand. "Thanks boys," he beamed with what he thought was a warm smile at them, and finished the previous glass before starting on the new one.

The smile actually, after the fourth pint, had become rather like that of a glassy eyed frog after a surfeit of flies. The froggy grin was beginning to turn into a vacuous and silly one, and he desperately cudgelled his brain for what to say.

He really had planned to do a burglary. His tales of what he got up to with Big Ernie were getting wilder and even he suspected the truth that no one believed them anymore, even if they had been inclined to believe them in the first place. And that was probably unlikely

Anyway Big Ernie was to be released soon and someone might tell him what they had overheard in the pub. Lofty, referred to as Lofts was called that because he was a rather weedy little man of about five foot five inches or less. Big Ernie was not the sort of man you went round telling tales about.

The little man had a constant dismal sounding cough, "like death warmed up," some person had remarked. It was the cough which did not make him a second or even a third choice as an accomplice in burglary. Big Ernie, however had a soft spot for men who were down on their luck, or so they claimed.

He had a year or so ago once accompanied Big Ernie and nearly got them both arrested when he had tried to climb onto a shed roof to get in at a bathroom window. The catch of the window had come undone rather more quickly than he had bargained for. He clung to it for a moment then it slipped through his hand and he crashed onto the shed roof, not quite going through and having to be got down by Big Ernie.

Ernie had half carried, half dragged him into the garden next door where he had lain half unconscious while Big Ernie legged it straight into the arms of a rather surprised policeman. Lofty had come to and staggered off home after Ernie found himself in the police cells.

Neither was Big Ernie very much bigger. He appeared even weedier than Lofty. But whereas Lofty seemed to have trouble even lifting his feet when he walked, Big Ernie was one of those Jack Russell type of men who was all energy and aggression. In prison he had made himself a reputation as a man to be wary of.

Lofty was worried about telling any more stories lest Ernie get to hear them and want to know why Lofts was always the hero in them and Big Ernie was cast in the role as the buffoon. Lofty was thinking of emigrating to somewhere like Manchester. He did not know where Manchester was but he knew it was 'up north somewhere' and a good distance from the south coast where Big Ernie was known to frequent.

"Yer!" he slurred for the third time. "Gorra nice little tickle goin." He paused, not for effect, but to take another gulp of his drink, and to think what next to say. The trouble was that his thoughts were as unsteady as his legs would have been if he had let go of the bar. His befuddle brain could not quite make out what the plan was. He did have on for someone else had put him on to it.

He began again, "thish 'oush I know." He waved an unsteady hand in the faces of his listeners in a vain attempt to stop them moving and went on. "They'm goin' on hhholi. Hol. Hol. Er, for their hol." He finished with what was intended as another expression of extreme secretiveness and cunning but which appeared to everyone else in the pub to be an impersonation of a fish flapping and flopping about on the bank of a river after the fisherman had brought it in to land.

Mow's humans did indeed intend having a holiday but having spent all their money on a new kitchen they had decided not to go away but simply stay at home and recline in the garden on sun loungers. She got in a stack of books from the Library. It was no longer called a library but a Discovery Centre which meant that children, on summer holiday from school ran around shrieking.

Mow's female human preferred libraries to be quiet so she could browse among the books and choose the ones she liked. Now she had to choose quickly and get them stamped so she could escape the noise of children and the inevitable deaf man with a loud voice explaining something to the librarian.

He, Mow's male human, did not read much so had stocked up for the holiday with several cases of real ale, some wine and a hidden cache of chocolate bars. His wife had forbidden him chocolate bars. She was fearful that he might become diabetic and she also made pointed remarks about his increasing waistline and the need for work in the garden. "It's getting overgrown out there," she would mutter and go on about rainforests and jungles.

At least the cat likes it he thought but did not dare say so. Mow did indeed like it. He could lurk under the rhubarb leaves and pounce out on birds or butterflies. He knew butterflies made him sick but he could not resist them. Like a kitten with a piece of string he simply had to leap at them and catch them with his claws. Having caught them the logical thing for an agile and perpetually hungry tomcat to do was to eat them.

"Disgusting!" snapped the woman and then spoiled it all by talking baby talk at him. "Oo is disgusting, does oo know that?" she asked in a silly voice tickling him where he liked to be tickled, under the chin.

Mow put up with the baby talk because tickling him under the chin was the sort of treatment he expected from the humans he owned. Stephanie the Staffordshire bull terrier was bewildered. "How can you swallow those nasty things?" She wrinkled her nose fastidiously as she said this. She was trying to
understand Mow and since not even cats understand cats, they just do not worry about it, However, she never would, she was a dog and neither dogs nor humans will ever be able to understand cats. .

Mow replied, "they flutter about so, I just cannot resist them. I'm addicted I guess," he said philosophically. He yawned and composed himself for another sleep but Stephanie insisted on talking. "Then there's all that hunting, all that catching birds and mice and," she made a face, "butterflies? Yuck!"

Mow stretched and yawned again. He turned the questioning on Stephanie something he always did when he did not want to answer. It always worked. "What about you?" Mow asked. "He'll get up and whistle and you'll both go off and he has you chasing that silly ball until he gets tired."

Stephanie thought about it and gave an answer which showed she was far more intelligent than Mow had given her credit for. "I hunt too," she said. "I heard him talking to that fat man next door and he said that dogs hunt in packs and run down the animal we want to eat."

Mow considered this and murmured sleepily, "so that's why you do all that barking whereas I am a stealthy hunter and try to make as little noise as possible."

Stephanie always gave credit where credit was due which Mow did not. He preferred to have the credit whether it was his due or not. This does have a bearing on the story which is about to unfold. Stephanie said admiringly, "you are very quiet, even I cannot hear you, I don't think there is another animal as quiet as cats can be, particularly yourself and you are a very big cat."

Mow licked his paw which was his way of preening himself though trying to appear modest. With an uncharacteristic sense of not wanting to appear just a little arrogant, Mow pointed out. "There is one creature who is the quietest of us all, have you not seen her?" Stephanie looked puzzled, "who's that?" she asked.

"The Barn Owl," said Mow. "You watch out over to the hedge round the field and the park at the back. When it gets dark she glides along the hedge like a ghost, like a wraith, silent as death." Stephanie listened wide eyed as Mow waxed poetic. "Not only are the owls completely silent but they catch more mice and voles in a few days than a cat could do in a month."

Stephanie positively goggled. "Do you mean that bird which make "whoo, whoo, whoo, noises?" she asked.

"That's a Tawny Owl," said Mow, "but they are much the same. Except that the barn owl has the most silent flight of all birds and of all hunters.

Stephanie was amazed at the encyclopaedic knowledge displayed by her feline friend. She still thought of Mow as a bit of a kitten, even though he was now full grown. She felt very proud of him like a human mother who has a son or daughter going off to university. Mow understood how it was best that a solitary, silent hunter, like himself had to know all about the other creatures who inhabited his territory.

There were those, like Stephanie, with whom he shared the house and the humans. She had shared food with him and mothered him when, as an ill-treated half grown cat, he had arrived on the doorstep and wormed his way into the female human's affections. He knew and respected the Owls and the Kestrels, he was wary of the stoats and the weasels and the badgers who lived in the rough ground between the field at the back and the park. The council kept it wild as a nature reserve but Mow knew nothing about councils or what they did.

Even when he and his arch rival, Tiger, the ginger tomcat, had ruined the cat and dog show and nearly caused a midterm election for the whole council, he was unaware of the uproar and upset they had caused. To a cat most human activity is irrelevant unless it involves food or directly affects them in some other way. This too has a bearing on what is to follow.

You might say that cats are selfish to a very high degree but that would be to attribute to them human feelings and emotions. Cats are simply, well, cats. They do not think like we do and they only see what is around them. If it does not directly affect them or if it cannot be eaten they may take a passing notice but they are not at all interested.

On the other hand, when, a few days later, Mow spotted a scruffy looking human hanging about and taking an undue interest in his house, Mow also took notice. In particular he noticed and remembered the smell. The scruffy human had a stale sort of smell, part body odour and part beer and pork scratchings.

It was his house, of course. That is how Mow understood things. The humans lived in the house and kept it warm for him to return to after he had inspected his territory, kept all the other cats in their places and checked on everything else as well as stopping to view anything unusual. That was why Mow noticed and observed the scruffy smelly man. That was why they had a sort of minor skirmish and why Mow stood his ground and the man made off, swearing to himself.

They say that cats are curious. Within certain limits they are. Noisy, smelly or violently moving things only annoy them. Some things like this, if they are very big even frighten them. All these things cats avoid if they can. Cats like peace and quiet, to sleep and to prowl the night looking for adventure and food. Like most animals and better than some, they are extremely sensitive and so loud noises, offensive smells and violently moving things worry them so they think all these are better avoided. Lofts was certainly smelly in an offensive way, he was not particularly loud not was he very fast but he like violence if it could be done to smaller people and to animals who did not appear to be able to be aggressive or to seem to be able to defend himself. His experience of cats was of course limited. He had never before come across a large tom cat like Mow. Nor for that matter one like Tiger the ginger tom.

You might think that cats are perpetually hungry. This is not true, only tame humans see animals in human terms. Cats are wild and have the instincts of the wild. They eat because, in the wild, there may be no food tomorrow. If they were human they would have, as a motto, "grab it while it is going" or better still, "before it hides," or "runs away".

So it was that Mow registered unusual behaviour on the part of the scruffy human. First he walked past the house. Then he stopped and looked back at it for some seconds. Then he walked slowly back and stopped to tie his shoelace. This in itself was suspicious since he wore slip on shoes with no laces. They also badly needed polishing. Mow approached the man who did not see him until Mow had stopped just out of reach, and looked at him.

Being stared at unblinkingly by a large and rather hostile looking tomcat is disconcerting to say the least. It was particularly disconcerting since the scruff felt a certain amount of guilt, bent as he was on mischief. If a policeman had looked at him like Mow was he would certainly have been very ill at ease. In a way it was worse having a large and unfriendly cat staring at him as if he knew all the devious, dirty and downright criminal thoughts going on in his mind.

The scruffy, smelly man did not like animals. Being, in his own estimation at least, a criminal, he could only think of dogs as guard dogs or police dogs and as cats as pussy cats he could bully. We already know that Mow was not a pussy cat. The man paused. There was something about Mow which made him uneasy. Mow for his part, being an extremely fastidious cat, was thinking, "what a disgusting smell!" Or it might have been better rendered into feline as, "Cor! What a truly nauseating pong!"

Seeing that Mow was smaller than he was the scruff decided to be brave and face Mow down. "Gerrrr!" he shouted. Then, "Gerroff! Scram!" He stamped his foot at Mow threateningly. At least it was meant to be a threat but Mow only saw it as pathetic. He bristled, His whiskers lay back on the side of his face, his fur stood on end and his tail began to flick to and fro. It started slowly but there was an energy about it which ought to have warned a more perceptive being than the scruff. Cats lash their tails when angry. Mow was angry. He had attacked humans before as when the youth up the road had tried to pull his tail when he was a year younger. That particular human kept out of Mow's way and Mow knew it.

The scruff stamped his foot again but Mow stood his ground and spat out a few swear words. When a cat like

Mow spits at you and swears in that abusive, insulting language all of its own you know you have trouble on your hands. The Scruff was even beginning to think that he ought to devise an honourable way out of the impasse. Usually when cats had got in his way he had threatened them and they had run off. That had given the Scruff a sense of power and he had enjoyed it for a few seconds.

Now a cat had stood up to him and looked ready to fight. He drew back, thought for a moment then, trying his best to put on a nonchalant air, turned and strolled away. He hoped the stroll expressed a sort of devil may care dignity but he only succeeded in looking like a mobile rag bag doing a spot of 'slinking away in defeat.'

Mow watched him then sauntered away to climb his favourite tree and to hide himself in the leaves among the branches. From his perch, hidden from the world among the leaves he watched that same world go by. It was quiet and restful and he snoozed, in that half awake, half asleep mode which cats adopt when they think something might happen. They would rather it did not happen, of course, but they would not want to miss it if it did, especially since it might be food.

Cats, by and large, are wild animals. Most dogs would not survive if they did not have humans to look after them. Most cats, however, would get on quite well though their diet would be less rich, and it would usually be running away and would have to be caught.

The humans were practicing for their holiday. You may have noticed that on the first day of a holiday humans look around and explore to work out what they are going to do. The women folk always want to see what the shops are like, the children want to rush straight onto the beach and into the water while the older men either want to drop into a deck chair or find a quiet pub.

The first day is always spent looking for these things. Mow's humans were relaxing on sun loungers. Their holiday was going to be different; they already had it planned, so they were doing it. She was reading a book, she had read it before but it had been a long time ago and she had forgotten the story so she was reading it again.

He was asleep, at peace with the world and content to be able to do nothing. It would not be for long however since earlier on he had eaten two chocolate bars and the wrappers had fallen out of his pocket onto the ground. The female human had spotted them. She was planning to use them for ammunition, not to fire at him or throw at him exactly but to point out again his need for exercise and the dangers of diabetic symptoms if he did not start work on the 'jungle' as she had got into the habit of calling it.

About tea time the female put down her book and started to make sandwiches. The male human stirred so she took the opportunity of lecturing him.
"What's in these sandwiches," he asked with a rather pointed look.
"Lettuce!" she answered.
"Lettuce? Nothing else?"

She answered in the negative pointing out that people who eat chocolate bars tend to get fat and put themselves in danger of heart attacks, hardening of the arteries and diabetic complications. Thus, she explained, he would have to go on a strict diet if he was to avoid all these unpleasant things.

"How is it that the cat gets anything it wants when it wants it and hasn't had any of these things?" "Mow climbs trees and goes off hunting and lots of other activities," she said, then added pointedly, "I haven't seen you climbing any trees lately."

Mow had just appeared, as if by magic, the moment the food had turned up. He was looking expectantly at the plates on a little table between the two sun loungers.
"You wouldn't like any of this," the male human told him.
Mow licked his lips and the female human said, "I've got something special for him."

Mow followed her to the kitchen door while the man shook his head sadly, muttering. "And I have to take second place to a piratical tom cat." The day, however ended quite pleasantly. The male human decided it might be diplomatic to attack 'the jungle' which he did with a garden fork. The female human went in did some clearing up and set about making an evening meal. Not lettuce this time but something more tasty.

Mow knew that his share would be put away safely for him. He watched as the humans got on with what they were doing and the male human took Stephanie out for her walk. It was more than a walk really because they would go off over the heathland and Stephanie would go running off looking for rabbits. Had she been a lurcher or a terrier she might have found some but she was not and she did not. Instead she ran round barking and then settled to running after an old cricket ball which the human threw away again as soon as she brought it back. This activity as you know disgusted Mow. To him it seemed pointless and subservient of her and he wondered how she could allow herself to wear a collar and be put on a lead for the walk through the heath of the town centre. He supposed it was to do with dogs hunting in packs but he still thought it an awful waste of time when any sensible animal could be sleeping.

He had come down from the tree and had decided, after his meal to go and topatrol his territory. He knew Ginger Tom was not allowed out at night. Indeed Ginger Tom was getting slow and fat. Since the fight in the marquee and the ensuing disaster his owner had made sure he stayed in at nights. He no longer posed a threat to Mow's rule over the local feline world.

As Mow slunk through the grass towards the park and the estate where some of his lady friends lived his thoughts disturbed him about the unpleasantly smelling man. He had a feeling they might meet again. This would be different to his meetings with Ginger Tom, otherwise known as Tiger, but not that much different.

Tiger had been an enemy he could respect since he was a rival for dominance. The man's attitude was also one of dominance where, on the first encounter Mow had prevailed, by frightening the man off. There the similarity ended. Mow did not respect scruffy or dirty people, nor those who behaved suspiciously. People or cats who behaved suspiciously he knew did so because they were up to something. Mow knew because he was usually 'up to something' himself.

People often think in beastly terms to describe something awful or inhuman like the Holocaust. The real beasts, the animals who share our world are not at all beastly in this sense. Mow was a predator; his nature was to eat small mammals and birds, even insects such as butterflies even though they made him sick. Mow was never intentionally cruel in the human sense of being cruel for its own sake and taking pleasure in it.

A cat fight may seem cruel in that pain is inflicted but animals avoid violent confrontations if they can. That is why there is always a lot of pre-fight posturing, growling and screeching. It saves injuries to both parties which might disable them. The cat who cannot screech the loudest of the protagonists, is smaller usually; it gives in and walks away knowing he does not stand a chance against a bigger fitter and more aggressive animal. This is sensible, it saves a lot of pain and suffering Cats are thus sensible. It is humans who are cruel who make animals and people fight for their amusement. It is also stupid of humans to act in these ways. It is humans who have wars and who blow each other up.

Some may argue that cats, "play" with their victims before killing and eating them. In the wild this is the way mother cats teach their kittens to hunt. By domesticating cats we tend to have made them more kittenish. The true wild cat is a much more fierce and cunning animal than even Mow.

As patrols go that night's work ended early and was fairly uneventful. All his friends seem to have been kept indoors by their humans. The owls were active and any small mammals which might have interested Mow were cowering out of reach and silent.

Mow crept back soon after midnight to become aware of a smell getting increasingly stronger. It was a familiar smell, a nasty smell with an overpowering odour of hops, yeast and an absence of soap and water. The would-be Mr. Big of crime, known whimsically as Lofts, had decided to pursue his career of villainy by burgling the house which Mow privileged by his presence. He was under the mistaken impression that the owners were away on holiday.

If cats have a sense of ownership it is a territorial one, though it is likely that they do not think in those ways at all. He was only mildly annoyed that his humans had not been made alert by the now overpowering smell. Human senses are dull unlike those of most animals and birds. The disgusting and revolting pong was coming closer all the time and getting more and more pungent. He wrinkled his nose in distaste and crept into his box where he could curl up and wrap his tail round his nose and mouth. He wondered whether Stephanie had noticed the smell, he felt sure she had. Mow could not sleep. He felt ill at ease. The origin of the smell had given him a sense of nastiness other than the smell.

Stephanie had indeed noticed the smell and was pacing the floor of the hallway sniffing and in a disturbed state of mind. The smell was unpleasant but it was a human smell. The male human often smelt like it after he had been to the pub. On the other hand she also sensed something unpleasant. It may have been instinct and her instinct would have been right.

The burglar, for now such he was since he had opened the side gate and let himself onto the passage alongside the house and so onto private property where he had no right to be, made an unsteady progress into the yard at the back. He realised that he was unsteady just as he had become aware earlier that he needed to fortify himself with alcohol in order to go through with his rather vague plans of burglary.

He could hardly back out, he had boasted earlier that he might be "out on a job, a nice little tickle". The phrase seemed to him to be the sort of jargon a real professional burglar might use. It gave him a sense of being a professional, which he was not or ever would be. He would not be able to show his face in the pub again if he failed. He could not use the weather as an excuse since the night was dry though dark with clouds that might have held promise of rain later.

Mow heard the scuffed steps coming round the passage and out onto the backyard and back garden. He lifted his head. By now all his senses were alert and he was ready for fight or flight. Slowly and cautiously he got to his feet and was aware of a pair of human feet getting closer towards his box. He crouched ready to spring, away from any threat if he could possibly make it into the open, or to attack if, as it seemed, he might be trapped in his box by the menace.

Mow's box seemed an ideal vantage point from which to work at the catch of the window. He stepped up onto the box so conveniently placed and was surprised to find the catch fitted so a gap was left for the air to circulate. With Stephanie in the house the humans had felt no fears about leaving it open a crack. With a screwdriver, the one bit of planning the apprentice crime boss was capable of, he levered the catch and prodded it free.

At that moment the box began to give way. It all happened in a couple of seconds, but Mow sprang out of the box as the man's foot crashed down onto his tail. With only his head inside the unfortunate burglar found himself losing his balance and being trapped by the very window he had tried to break in by. His ears caught on the window and pulled it back trapping him by his head. The window had been pulled to and it say across his neck. His top end was stuck in the window and his legs were trapped by the wreckage of Mow's box.

At that moment an unpromising criminal career was cut off and stopped forever. Indeed when he finally had his day in court it was not the censure of the magistrate, nor the sentence of more community service which he was given, but the shame of being the holder of the title of 'the world's most unsuccessful burglar'. What really mortified him and ended for ever a career which had hardly begun were the gales of laughter that echoed round the court. The humiliation finally convinced him that a life outside the law was not for him. Robin Hood he was not, nor ever would be, nor was he Al Capone though he had long aspired to be something of that sort.

The growl of an angered Staffordshire bull terrier is an awesome thing. He fell into blind panic fighting to get himself free from the window which held his head fast as if in a vice. Alas it was useless to try for at the same time he was also attempting to wave his legs in the air to avoid another deadly attack.

If Stephanie's appearance struck terror into him it was increased enormously by the banshee screech of rage accompanied by needle sharp and powerful teeth and claws which attacked his leg, shredding his trousers and drawing blood.

Cats are very proud of their tails. With them they express all sorts of emotions from pleasure to curiosity to sheer demented rage. It was this latter that motivated Mow.

Normally very fastidious, he would have avoided at all costs the garments and the body of the noxious human who had his head trapped and who had demolished his box. On this occasion that human had trodden on his tail and that simply had to be avenged, swiftly and terribly.

Caught between the teeth of a bull terrier bared only inches from his face, accompanied by menacing snarls, and the demon who was mincing and mangling his legs with razor sharp claws, the burglar was in a state of blind terror. He felt hope surge into his heart when he heard the sound of sirens rapidly approaching. Perhaps that ought to be that the 'failed' burglar was relieved by the arrival of the police and an ambulance which the male human had called on his phone.

Fortunately for the failed burglar they arrived quickly. Indeed he literally fell into the arms of the constable who had answered the call as that officer levered the window away from Loft's head. The policeman's colleague remarked that it looked as if he were greeting a long lost brother. It had, for once, been a quiet night down at the local nick and at casualty for a change. The police and the paramedics got plenty of laughs back at their respective canteens when they told the story of the burglar who had been arrested by a cat and a dog.

As for Lofts his misery was increased by the news that 'Big' Ernie had been released from prison early for 'good behaviour' if you can believe it, and was to be part of his gang on community service. "Allo Ole Lofts," had been his greeting when finally they met, "I bin opin to see yer agin!"

MOW AND THE GHOSTS

The vicar's wife slipped out of bed, there was noise outside. It was like swarms of bees were having a carnival. There were separate men's and women's voices too. Some of these were being raised but the shouts sounded indistinct against the background of the noise of vehicle engines, other quieter conversations and a general crash and rattle of equipment. As she drew back a corner of the bedroom curtain her jaw dropped and her eyes widened in surprise and horror. "Sam!" she called. Then more urgently, "Sam!"

A muffled voice from under the duvet made a sort of groaning sound. It was the vicar who tended these days, having left the Marines and taken up the cloth, to enjoy his sleep and to have difficulty rousing himself. At seven he went over to the church to pray and then returned, usually sooner than he should, for his breakfast. It was nothing like seven, more like six when his wife woke him from a comfortable sleep.

She, never a patient sort of person at the best of times, grabbed a handful of the duvet and pulled. "Wha? Wha? It's cold," he complained, trying to grab the duvet. She was insistent, "come and look!" she demanded. "Must I?" he said, then as his bare feet touched the cold floor he muttered, "Oh! Hell!" This of course in some quarters would have been considered very unvicarly. His wife glared at him and, jabbing with her finger towards the window said in a commanding voice. "Look! Out there, it's a circus."

She did not mean, of course one with a big top, performing animals, acrobats and clowns. He, being slow on the uptake at six in the morning, wondered what a circus was doing in his small front garden. As he staggered round the bed and over to the window he tried to think how a circus could be set up on his front lawn.

He gave up and followed his wife's pointing finger where he saw a crowd of people all milling round with various vehicles almost blocking the, once quiet, road in which they lived. Some of the people, men and women, had notebooks, some had video equipment. Some were simply rushing about like the proverbial headless chickens attempting to set things up and getting in each other's way. Still others were shouting into microphones while their assistants waved their arms. He began to see why his wife had referred to it all as a circus.

Utterly dazed he turned to her and asked, "how did it all get here? Where did it come from?" Her reply was even less vicar's wifely and contained several swear words. How the ___ ___should I know? Maybe you invited them." The vicar gave her a puzzled look. "Me? Why would I invite them? Anyway what are they doing on our front lawn?" By this time she was beginning to calm down a little and replied in a cooler voice. "It looks to me as if they're interviewing the paper boy."

There was indeed a crisply dressed young lady hurriedly scribbling down what a pimply looking youth was saying to her in answer to her questions. The young lady patted the youth on the back and smiled triumphantly at him. She was an up and coming reporter for one of the prestigious news agencies and was pleased with herself. Always interview the youngsters first, was her motto, particularly the gormless ones. It never failed.

The completely vacuous young man, having leaned his bike against the hedge, had been spellbound by the young reporter's charm and her stunning good looks. With a few well-chosen remarks she had him like putty in her hands, so to speak. Soon she had him telling tales of the supernatural, the occult, and Satanic rituals conducted in the church. It was all stuff she put into the naïve youth's mind in the first place. That, however, did not matter to a journalist of her ambition and imagination, it was the story that mattered, and if the story was mostly fiction, so much the better.

And it was just the beginning. All she had to do was to polish up the story a bit and it would make the readers of the early evening editions shake in their shoes with their hair, if they had any, standing on end. She was beginning to feel pleased with herself, but even at her comparatively young age, she was not one to rest on her laurels. The story had to be good for some days before she went on to report the next lurid sensation. She intended to be doing a lot more digging among the more superstitious and impressionable members of the community.

Other reporters were similarly engaged in capturing old gentlemen tottering down to the newsagents and extracting from them something more exciting to garnish and tell to their readers, listeners or viewers. Meanwhile more vehicles with even more masses of technical equipment and coils and coils of wire were drawing up to be unloaded into any available space as close to the vicar's garden as they could get. Other people of the journalistic circus, which was rapidly becoming a journalistic feeding frenzy, were fanning out towards the town centre.

Some enterprising reporters had gone round the corner to the church. A few of the more eager souls were peering in through the windows at the front and side or looking round the graveyard.

No one thought of asking the vicar, or his lady for an interview. After all they were not likely to confess to anything exciting like black Satanic rituals and sacrificing chickens, or even people on the church altar at midnight. All they wanted were some pictures of them looking stunned and suspiciously sinister as they stepped out to question what all the fuss was about.

The vicar made his escape through the back door and the back alley which took him to the church, leaving his wife to face the inquisition if she felt up to it. As a Marine he had faced being shot at quite fearlessly but this he could not face, he left it to the more fearsome of the species, his womenfolk. He knew full well that his wife could deal with the media people. She was highly articulate and quick thinking which, at six in the morning he was not.

The reporters there were still peering in at windows, a few videoed the building and the graveyard or took pictures on expensive and complicated looking digital cameras. More reporters were inspecting the graveyard more thoroughly than a police forensics team looking for clues to murder.

However you cannot get a lot of sense from a building, however sinister you may try to make it look in a picture. It is a waste of journalistic time trying to talk to buildings. People are much better, the more gullible they are the better they are as fodder for the more sensational of the national news corporations.

Very few people knew of the little back door which led into the stoke hole in the days when the verger had to light a furnace and stoke it with coke. That was all gone and gas central heating was used instead. However the stoke hole had its uses, mostly by the verger, a retired gardener, who kept the weeds down in the graveyard. The vicar knew of it and had a key so he could go into the church without being buttonholed by anxious parishioners.

He had soon found out, as a curate, that old ladies wanting to gossip for hours on end find a cleric very useful since they cannot say things like, "Shut up! You garrulous old bat. Go and annoy someone else." You had to listen politely, sometimes for ages and pretend you enjoyed listening to their tales which they had probably told you before.

Access to the church was gained, from the stoke hole, up some steps and through a small door into his vestry. It was much better than going in at the front and so announcing that you were in attendance so that parishioners with problems could find you. No one else knew of it unless you observed a certain cat stalking through the churchyard followed by two or three feline female admirers. They, one after the other, followed Mow who jumped, up onto a covered rainwater barrel then onto a window ledge. They then seemed to disappear, as if dematerialising, through a closed window at the back of the church.

The window was not really closed but the catch tended to slip however hard the verger tried to force it closed. The catch just slipped off and the window would swing either way. Mow learned to lean his weight on it and it would give way for him to push through the window. Seen from the outside one would only have noticed a closed window and nobody bothered to try to push the window to see if it was secure.

You will have guessed, by this time that it was our hero and his feline followers who were the reason for all the fuss outside the vicarage that autumn morning. How it came about was as I am about to try to explain. Needless to say Mow himself was totally unaware of the confusion and excitement he was the innocent cause of.

Mow was on one of his forays off into the wider world. It was in the very early hours and Mow had visited the area which people who know these things would have said was his territory. Mow usually avoided the area of the town preferring the housing estates which had grown up round what was once a very small country town. The shopping precinct, the offices and restaurants, which, over the years had also taken over what once were rows of terraced houses, held no great interest for Mow. Not, that is, until late at night or in the early hours.

During the day and the evening it was too noisy and too dangerous. He only visited the town centre when everyone else was asleep and only the odd policeman and a few cats roamed, fully alert for what may come or the possibility of food or adventure.

The churchyard was backed onto on the other side from the alley which ran past the vicarage, by a block of shops and restaurants. There was also a car park where a burger van catered for late night revellers. These of course were of interest for Mow since they were a source of discarded uneaten food. He turned his nose up at the exotic smells at the rear of the Indian restaurant and the Chinese takeaway. He did, however find the bins behind Charley's Retro Café and the environs of the burger van, well worth investigating. It really was called by people, Charley's Caff and Charley, there really was one, who, as a chef, was a proper Charley, He also catered also for late night revellers.

These were usually well tanked up and so were not too particular what they ate, or were too drunk to realise its potential for gastric convulsions. Even so such convulsions were usually blamed on the alcohol they had consumed. Food was often discarded around the car park, or careless 'night owls' dropped it all over the place. The area consequently, became a meeting place for cats, the odd fox or two and some rats and mice who often also became food for the night-prowling predators. This was mostly during the early hours after midnight and well after the last humans had retired. It was also before the early ones were awake.

Mow had been curled up asleep, with one eye half open, on an armchair which had seen better days. It had belonged to a man who lived over his shop and he had put it out intending to take it to the tip since the dustmen had refused to take it away. He always reminded himself to take it but always found other things more important to do.

Mow thought he had, very kindly, left it out for him. Very obliging some of these humans, he thought. No other cats challenged his right to sleep there since, after frequent use it became saturated with his scent. And Mow's scent suggested his possible near presence. No other cat dared, even in their wildest dreams to challenge Mow's right to sole possession of the discarded arm chair.

The vicar had, one morning, as usual, walked up the alley and to the door of the stoke hole. He was surprised to see a large black and white, rather smart looking tom cat. "Hello" Puss," he greeted Mow. Mow responded by telling him what his name was, though the vicar, being human did not understand though he did stroke Mow and tickle him under the chin. Mow responded by purring and rubbing himself against the man's legs.

As is usual on these occasions when man meets cat there is a total lack of understanding on the part of the human. Mow simply saw him as a useful contact. He was clearly feline friendly and so was probably good for food, for providing it that is, not for eating himself. That is exactly what he did, providing food and attention for hungry cats. The vicar thought that Mow liked him and that rubbing against his leg was a cat's way of showing it. Liking did not enter into it. You might as well have said that Blackbeard the pirate liked heavily laden merchant ships. Mow was, as are all cats, an individualist and an opportunist; he was marking his territory and saying, this soppy man who wears a long black frock, has now paid me homage and, in all likelihood, will provide me with the good things in life, or at least access to them.

The scent he put on the man also said, "Beware! This man belongs to Mow, befriend him at your peril!" Access there was and Mow followed the vicar into the church. The vicar was under the impression that Mow had become attached to him. This, in a sense was right, though not as the vicar believed. The vicar, as an ex-marine was a push over for cats. Marines are soldiers who go to sea. They are an extremely macho corps and as all men of a macho lifestyle, they admire and like all animals but, like the sailors they serve with, have a soft spot, in particular, for cats. Mow was well in, with his feet under the table, so to speak, all four of them.

Mow sat on a comfortable hassock, while the vicar knelt and talked to someone. Some people might have been bewildered by this sort of behaviour, others might have mocked unless they had known that the vicar had once been a Marine. Mow simply saw it as another example of human behaviour which was often strange and not easily explained but which a wise cat tolerates as long as the humans pay the proper tribute to their feline friend. If they do not then, of course, the feline is no longer a friend and makes himself scarce.

Mow followed the vicar as he got up and left the church by the same way he had come in. He followed him all the way home. "Don't go bringing stray cats in here," snapped his wife who really liked animals but who knew that if she did not put her foot down, her husband, who was a soft hearted man, would invite every stray animal, homeless tramp and not a few layabouts, in for meals. That is for meals she would have to provide.

"He's not a stray," he pointed out, "he's in too good a condition; anyway I smelt mice in the church and if he follows me in for my devotions then I will have had at least one convert in this centre of atheism and godlessness."

His wife could not help laughing, "Saint Samuel of Assisi? I think not! You're not the sort to go preaching to the animals and birds."

"I might as well," he answered for all the interest I get in this place. Anyway," he went on, "what have you done with the bacon rinds." She sighed, knowing that the handsome tom cat sitting licking its lips on her kitchen doorstep had him completely besotted.

"Over there on top of the bin. I just knew, sooner or later, you would find some animal to feed." She shook her head despairingly. Mow gratefully received the homage in the gracious way a monarch receives gifts from a foreign prince by the hand of an ambassador. He sniffed the hand that was holding out the rinds and then took them in his mouth and crunched them up. Satisfied, and without a backward glance, he stalked off knowing there were more where those came from. He made his way back to the church.

The vicar would have been surprised and his wife cynical, for he stopped beneath the window of the stoke hole and, thinking it was worth investigating, leapt up via the lid of the water butt onto the window sill and sniffed at the glass. It moved; Mow pushed with his head and it moved again. Mow leaned his weight upon it and it opened and Mow jumped in from the window onto a conveniently placed chair and then onto the floor.

From the floor of the stoke hole he proceeded up the steps into the vestry and then into the main body of the church. He smelt mice and he was aware of the large numbers of hassocks and the pews which would guarantee a draught free sleep to a tired cat. Later on Mow left by the same way as he had entered. He felt a deep sense of satisfaction at a good night's work well done. The next night he returned with Shadow and Muriel two of his lady friends.

Shadow was a pedigree cat with the pedigree name of Night Shadow Moon Lady. The human she owned was deeply into ancient religious practices and the more recent applications of them. One had to admit that the name was appropriate for Shadow was a dark blue-grey colour who conducted herself regally as though conscious, which she was not, of a long line of aristocratic ancestry.

Muriel was what Shadow aspired to be, that is an alley cat. Muriel aspired to be what Shadow was, an aristocratic looking feline, who looked as if she had a long pedigree. Both cats felt that Mow, as a handsome and very large tom cat with piratical instincts, was a suitable male escort to be seen with and to hunt with. They also admired his singing which may have had something to do with the circus that morning, a week and some days later, in front of the vicarage.

Things, as things are wont to do; settled themselves into a routine. Shadow and Muriel seemed to have attracted a collection of other assorted cats, including less dominant males and neutered ones. They played games in the church, they hunted mice until every mouse, every rat and every squirrel in the vicinity of the church and the churchyard had emigrated to a less hostile environment. Or had come to a swift and savage end and been eaten. Well you would, wouldn't you if you were to be hunted by a conglomeration of hungry cats.

It was a conglomeration and not a pack. Only dogs go in packs. Certainly there was an alpha male and Shadow was the alpha female but the other cats came and went as they felt like it. Indeed Mow was not flattered by the crowding of his special place by lesser felines. Indeed were it not for a regular offering of bacon rinds, leftover sausage and meat scraps to which he and the lady cats were treated he would have abandoned the place altogether. As it was he felt a bit annoyed that all the other, lesser cats had found his secret of the way into the church by means of the wonky window.

A lot of singing went on. There was some quarrelling among the lesser beings of the feline world and one evening the place was invaded by Tiger the Ginger Tom who had surmised that something was going on. He knew nothing about it and as an ex-alpha male, in his reckoning an existing alpha male, he needed to find out what it was. What it was, was Mow, his fur bristling and his tail beginning to flick from side to side in an outraged display of anger at the invasion, by a rival, of his domain.

Now the two large tom cats who faced each other in the middle of the church were not the same as the two who had fought each other to a standstill in the marquee at the cat and dog and pet show months before. Mow was fully grown; he had filled out with powerful muscle. He had been muscular even then but now even more so. He was also in the peak of condition. An active life of tree climbing, exploring, fighting and hunting ensured all that. He also had a rich and varied diet which kept him in health and fitness.

Tiger, on the other hand, ever since the disaster at the cat and dog show, had been kept in. He still had his rich diet provided for him by a besotted female human. Sadly he was slightly overweight due to his enforced lack of activity and the diet he was kept on.

The fight went on for some time. There was a preliminary musical work up to a pitch of anger when the two cats became a revolving ball of furiously indignant fur. They broke apart to continue the fight with defiance and some closer attention to tactics. Tiger's lack of condition eventually had the effect of wearing him down. Mows attacks grew more furious as he felt his adversary weakening and Tiger, at last defeated, made off in terror down into the stoke hole and up onto the ledge and out of the window.

He had not reckoned on the water butt outside the stoke hole. Its wooden lid had supported even the weight of Mow on it as, from time to time, he had used it to launch himself up to the window. Tiger crashed down onto it with

Mow, still spitting defiance and terrible threats from the window sill. The lid split into two halves and Tiger was plunged ignominiously into the water. He howled and spat as he climbed out and made off through the churchyard determined never to visit Mow's territory again.

So it was that, on that particular night, two of the town drunks, there were several who competed regularly for that unenviable title, were supporting one another on their way home. As one collapsed the other hauled him to his feet saying, "come on! you drunken sot, you can't sleep here." The other would make some comment, allow himself to be dragged to his unsteady feet and the one who had so dragged him then seemed to swoon with the effort and, in his turn, collapse. In this way they made very slow progress. Even had they known where they were going they would have taken all night. As it was they intended to get to an estate on the other side of the town and would never have arrived since they were going in entirely the wrong direction.

Passing, or rather collapsing next to the churchyard on that particular night that the great Mow v Tiger bout was shortly due to take place, they decided to take a rest. "Lesh 'ave a resht," one said to the other. The other agreed and both men managed to stagger into the churchyard. The lights of a police car made then stagger faster to find safety behind the church, funnily enough quite near the stoke hole where Tiger had just found himself and was about to confront Mow.

The two were about to nod off when an unearthly blood chilling noise came from the stoke hole. It seemed to but when they looked up it came from all around them. They sat up, well one did, the other tried to then collapsed again. Both were terror struck. Had you been able to see in that dark churchyard you would have seen extreme horror was written all over their faces. At that moment the eerie, unearthly noise started up again, louder than ever.

At the same time, two small black cats quickly dived out through the window and raced off to find their way home. The drunks failed to see the cats properly in the dark but they did see black shapes and the movement of their passing as they swished through the long grass which the verger had omitted tocut the day before..

There were more fearful noises, soft and ghostly music filled the air than it turned to more violent outraged shrieking as if the demons themselves were out and about, as indeed the two inebriates concluded.

"Sho yer she shir." The man broke off his story to look pleadingly at the reporter who, hearing him remark how story telling was thirsty work, put his hand in his pocket for the price of yet another pint. "Me an me friend was takin' a short cut. It were at the back of the church." "Near the alley," prompted the reporter, who was buying the drinks for one of the two who had been terrified almost into sobriety that night in the churchyard.

"Yersh!" answered the man who was already beginning to slur his words, We saw two black shapes, evil they were, they run through the wall of the church and flew towards us. Then there was these noishesh. All ghashtly and ghoshtly, like they was demons from hell after us."

"What did you do?" asked the young reporter.

"We ran," answered his witness, "wiv all the demonsh in hell at our tail we ran and ran an we collapshed outside the pub and the landlady took us in an' revived us."

"Oh dear!" said the reporter to himself it sounds as if they made it up in order to get revived, it was very convenient to collapse outside a pub, even if it had been closed for an hour or more.

His editor, the editor of the local paper felt that the Weekly Journal was standing still, it needed, he had thought, something to revive its falling readership and a few sensational stories would help. He had sent out his two journalists both in their first job to find exciting and sensational stories. They found them. They found as many stories as there were drunks, layabouts and thirsty folk to tell them.

Both had come across rumours that funny things were going on in the church,
both, but separately, had come across the two who had been in the churchyard that night and had heard the shrieks, the moans and screams and had seen, so they said, some demonic beings. They were now in separate pubs lubricating the tongues and the imaginations of their two garrulous and thirsty witnesses.

So it was that the editor went slightly over the top in publishing a story that there were ghostly goings on at the church when all respectable people were at home in bed.

The police denied any such goings on but were a little uneasy for they too had found men, usually men up to no good, who told tales of mysterious happenings. The rumours grew and the articles in the Journal added a lot of fuel to the fires which were already alight in the imaginations of the townspeople.

To the editor's delight he soon found the big national papers and the television taking an interest. His paper came out with even bigger headlines. "Satanism, is it alive and well in our peaceful town?" asked one headline. Others proclaimed. "More Mystery at Parish Church," and, "Demonic Developments What is our vicar up to?"
All went quiet for a couple of days. The Editor of the paper was planning an even bigger exposure of the depravity which had invaded the Church of England. The vicar had phoned the editor to protest but the editor had the journalistic bit between his teeth and was determined to wring out of the story the maximum amount of mileage. Then, as the bigger regional and national newspapers got wind of the story, the feeding frenzy of journalists interviewing everyone in the town began.

Interviewees included all those known to be short of a brain cell or two and those with a predilection for strong drink since these were known to be more suggestible and more easily persuaded to claim outrageous and spectacular visions. One had had a genuine experience which was, however, quite unnerving so that he was never quite the same again.

"Them eyes!" he shuddered at the memory. "They was all staring at me. I was just curious, you know, like yer do. I looked through the window to see if there really was anything there and suddenly all these eyes." He paused for another good shudder and then went on. "They was all looking at me, 'orrible it was, they just stared, never blinked or nothin' just stared then all sort er, went out."

"Went out?" queried the reporter.

"Yer!" answered the intellectually challenged gentleman. He gave a thirsty glance at his interrogator to see if he would take the hint and added, "demonic it was." Had the reporter bothered to check at night he would have found that cars coming to the roundabout near the church invariably shone their lights so that the church, while not exactly illuminated, yet was lit enough to make the eyes of cats reflect an unblinking stare, at anyone trying to see through the windows nearest the road. The cats themselves were in darkness but their eyes shone eerily in the headlights of cars. It would have appeared to anyone looking in as if he were being stared at by a gathering of ghouls or a coven of demons, denizens of the deepest hell, meeting to plan the destruction and damnation of the population of a once quiet and unassuming country town. And its worried and unassuming vicar who was wondering what all the fuss was about.

Rumours grew and became more outrageous. Another 'witness' of the depravity of the vicar insisted to yet another reporter that it was the wild hunt itself ranging across the sky and plunging downwards to scoop up the souls of the damned from the churchyard or from the church itself below.

This was confirmed by a drinking pal of the witness who claimed that two of the worst people in the town had died earlier that night and, no doubt, the Devil had come to claim his own. The stories went on and on and grew and grew with the telling.

A chauffeur driven limousine drew up further down the street from the where the medea circus was still in full swing. A dignified patrician looking gentleman emerged and walked along to stop at the vicarage and then to ring the bell.

"It's the bishop."

"Don't be daft."

"It is."

"Then let him in before he freezes to death."

The vicar certainly felt in need of support. The circus was still busy outside though some of the reporters had gone.

He opened the door to be greeted with, "hello Sam, now I know there is no such thing as bad publicity but don't you think this is taking things a bit too far?" Sam was relieved to see that the Bishop was smiling as he said this.

The Bishop was ushered inside while the vicar's wife made coffee and sought out the brandy they had left over from last Christmas and which she had put aside for a special occasion. This had not turned out to be the sort of special occasion she had in mind but she felt they all might be in need of all the help they could get. Indeed, they stood in need of all the help and something stimulating that happened to be going. They had to make do with just half a bottle of brandy, but it seemed to do the trick and the Bishop was laughing merrily as they concluded that cats were invading the church and were the cause of all the trouble. "The verger told me that he could never fasten the window properly," he explained to the Bishop, who laughed some more.

Meanwhile Mow was curling up for a sleep on his favourite chair, the one usually occupied by his male human. He felt happy and content. Full of pilchard, he was blissfully unaware of the confusion and excitement he had unintentionally caused. Had he been aware of it he would only have waggled his whiskers as if shaking off something sticking to them and concluded that humans were incorrigibly daft and incapable of rational cat-like behaviour.

More Books by Roger Penney
Published by CRF Publishers

More First Century Close-Ups.
Dry Bones
The Republic of Plato: A Simple Man's Guide
The Last days of Socrates: A Simple Man's Guide
Herod, Statesman, Ruler and Builder
Meetings and Encounters
The Girl on a Bus and Other Stories,
First Century Close-Ups, published by Crossbridge Books.
2005.
Nietzsche; A Simple Man's Guide.
Poems of Earth Sky and Beyond.
If Not You.
The Afterlife.
Jesus in Islam.
The Minor Prophets: Volume One
The Minor Prophets: Volume two.
The Seven Parables of the Kingdom.

Printed in Great Britain
by Amazon